CONFESSIONS

AND TIPS OF A

BLACK

GIRL ONCE LOST

(BASED ON A TRUE STORY)

Written By:

DARCELL D. MARSHALL

This book is dedicated to:

Darcell Marshall (Mom)

Dekirah Marshall

Anthony, Anthony Jr., Gianna
Marshall

And all the men, women, boys and
girls who are lost. Whenever you are ready
to be found, I pray that you gain the courage
to stand up for yourself and get out of the
streets as safely as possible.
And to ANYONE who is thinking
about getting involved with the game, please
use this book as a guide so that YOU DO
NOT make the same mistakes that I have.
You have been warned.

CONFESSION AND TIP NUMBER ONE:

IF SOMEONE TELLS YOU THAT YOU ARE CRAZY BELIEVE THEM, BUT MOST IMPORTANTLY DON'T FORGET TO PLAY THE PART

It was the year of 2003 that I officially became lost. At thirteen years old I had already lost my virginity, started smoking cigarettes and had gained curiosity about the streets and what it had to offer. I grew up in a family that consisted of my older sister and brother, myself and a single mother.

I was born in Thomasville NC but because we moved almost twice a year every year, I am from a little bit of everywhere. Our family was the usual "hood" type, lost and on welfare like many other black broken families here in

America. Of course, we had food stamps and a mother who was just as lost as we were, so you can only imagine the things that we had to go through and face growing up.

I've never had the flyest clothes or was never the most popular in school and was more of a loner than anything growing up and was even classified by my peers and family as being weird.

I've never had a role model or someone to show me anything other than the streets and how to survive or even a shoulder to cry on and talk to other than my brother and sister. We were left alone to fend for ourselves most of our lives while our mother was out running the streets and as she would call it "living her best life because you only live once."

So, all we had was ourselves rap videos and for my brother video games. Our family was based out of Paterson NJ and surrounding areas and that is where my brother and I spent our summers with my dad.

My sister however, was left alone during the summer months learning and growing in the streets. Eventually we all got tired of my mom's unstableness, daily rants, mental and physical abuse, ridiculous rules and strictness and tried to each find our way out of what we had known most of our lives to be a hell hole.

I was thirteen years old and we were living in Elizabeth NJ when it all got real for me. My mom had kicked my sister out of the house over a rumor of a boy and she had gone to live with my grandmother and eventually back to NC with my grandfather all by herself. My brother had found his way out by going to live with my father in Mahwah NJ and he never looked back.

So here I was all alone to deal with the abuse and loneliness this time without my brother and sister at thirteen years old with no friends and was moving back to NC to start my third school in the same school year.

Once we were back in NC, I made a promise to myself that I would no longer be the quiet girl with my mom and I will not take her abuse. So, once we were settled in and the stress hit her, she started with the abuse and I started with what she calls "acting out."

I felt so smothered with worry, stress and hatred towards my mother with no outlet and nowhere to turn to other than the streets. I barely ever got a chance to speak to my sister because she had already started stripping and my brother was in NJ trying his best to listen to my father and avoid the negativity that came from my mother.

I eventually started skipping school which turned into meeting older men and exchanging sex for a place to stay and some meals as I called myself running away from home. I would eventually get caught and end up having to go to Juvie for a weekend where I would learn even more ways on top of what was taught to me from my sister on how to survive and how to get money by tricking with older men and using them for everything that they had.

I ended up doing this for a while and instead of them releasing me back home, I had to go to group homes and on occasion mental institutions. I would stay for a week or two to see if I could entertain the thought of going back to school, graduating or eventually going back home to deal with my mother and her drama.

I choose to continue to hit the streets and be just like or even better than the strippers and tricks that I had learned to love. I had even tried to go and stay with my father in NJ for a year, but I was so messed up, lost and confused it didn't work out and I had to move back to NC with my mom.

There was one time that I ran away, and it changed my life forever. I ended up being released to a group home in High Point NC where I met my trifling match. There was an African girl who lived there with her baby and she decided to come into my room and steal from the little bit of things that I had owned.

I had gotten a pocket knife from one of my then sugar daddies and once I seen her walking around with my shirt on, I didn't think twice about smacking her with my knife. I almost cut her, and I would have had it not been for the staff breaking up the incident.

The police were called, and I was hauled off to Juvie and this time, I was going to be gone for a while. I was charged with assault with a deadly weapon but because I was only fifteen I was charged as a juvenile and was sent to what they called training school for six months.

While I was there I learned absolutely nothing but more ways on how to not get caught and what was going on in other places in NC in the streets. Unfortunately for me, I ended up spitting on a correctional officer and ended up with another charge, malicious conduct by a prisoner but this time I was sixteen and was charged as an adult and had to be on probation for 5 years.

Once I was released, I ended up moving back in with my mom. My sister had gotten into a very bad car accident and had to move back in with my mom while she healed. I was happy to walk out of those gates and see my sister standing there. Even though she was in a lot of pain and I couldn't touch her. I had finally had a reason to stay home and deal with my mom's drama.

Over the years she had grown a little (or so I thought) and it wasn't that bad this time around. My sister had in fact changed and I found that we were not as close as we use to be, but she had some money saved from dancing and was helping my mom pay bills and she also provided me with clothes and kept my hair done while I was home.

I eventually stated going to a local community college and begin working on getting my GED. I didn't think that I would be able to go back to regular school without being too embarrassed, so I opted for this option. I was close to getting my GED and had even started a part time job at Wendy's and was learning to get along with my mom (or so I thought) and my sister until she finally healed and was getting ready to move out again.

I eventually got tired of walking to work and school and called myself trying to get my mom to take me to work and school. Of course, I was denied and for some reason it was like I had a flashback of everything that had happened in the past.

I began to get refueled with anger and resentment all over again because it I was barely making any money and even though I was living with my mom I wasn't getting any support. Once again, I was smothered with stress and worry and all alone with no one to express myself to or turn to for guidance and support.

I had to deal with my mom constantly throwing in my face the fact that I was on parole and "play with her if I want to my ass will be back in jail" and being called crazy and weird on the regular bases.

I called myself venting to my next-door neighbor about the things that was going on and how I felt and of course she voiced her opinion to my mom. My mom called herself punching me once she found out what I had did and I ended up swinging back and it felt good! I was finally releasing all that hatred and everything that I had pent up inside of me for over a year.

My sister heard us fighting and she had the nerve to jump in and they jumped me. I had never felt so hurt in my life! I began crying and yelling and they eventually backed off.

But before I could look up, I was in handcuffs and had been sent to county jail and left with nowhere to go. My mom ended up pressing charges on me and I eventually had to do thirty days in High Point Jail and I was charged as an adult, so it was on my record along with the malicious conduct by a prisoner. Little did we all know, that was the last time that I would see or talk to my family for years!

After I served my time my, probation officer met me at the gate and told me that my mom wouldn't allow me to come back home and I had to go to yet another group home. Here I was, seventeen years old, no family, no unconditional love or support, no understanding, a criminal record, had been in and out of jail and group homes for the past four years and basically no hope what so ever.

Once I got into the group home I didn't hesitate to run away to a trick house that I had known from one of my previous run-ways.

I was three months shy of being eighteen, and I just knew that I would be able to live in the streets and make just enough until my birthday when I would be legal, and I could get my own public housing apartment and restart my life once again according to no one else's rules.

He had allowed me to stay with him but told me that no one could know that I was there because I was underage, and I had needed to find somewhere else to go before the week was out. I had no clothes and no idea what I was going to do.

I ended up calling a sex hot line and meeting a guy form NY named Q. He was about 45 years old and had his own place and wanted me to come over and have dinner. He came and picked me up and, in my mind, I was practicing telling him my version of what was going on and why I couldn't go home.

Of course, I told him that I was 20 and had just run out of luck and was looking to go back with him to NY. He agreed, and his first question was how I was going to make money to support myself. I hadn't thought that far to answer the question, so I told him that I didn't know. He quickly gave me his version on how we both could become rich in NY and it was pretty much what I had been doing all along, selling pussy but this time it was for way more money and I would be walking the streets and turning tricks in cars.

I didn't care. I had nowhere to go and charges that I had needed to get away from so that I wouldn't go to prison. He wanted to "sample" the goods so we eventually had sex. The next day he took me to Walmart and bought me a sweater dress, some high heels, lingerie and even a long clip on ponytail to "work" in.

He quickly schooled me on what to do, how to walk, how to talk, and how to watch out for the police and what blocks to stay on and what to do if I had someone trying to kidnap me or rape me, otherwise known as a "bad date." Later on that night he instructed me to shave everything and get dressed. Before I knew it, I was downtown Greensboro walking up and down the streets, in and out of cars turning trick after trick with no fears but only ambition to make as much money as possible so I could get far away from everything that I was running from.

By the end of the night I had made over $600 and Q finally said the words that I had wanted to hear. Let's book your trip to NYC for tomorrow.

CONFESSION AND TIP NUMBER TWO:

EVERYTHING THAT GLITTERS COULD REALLY BE GOLD. ITS UP TO YOU TO DECIDE IF YOU WANT TO FIND OUT IF ITS REAL

The next morning as promised I was on a one-way Grey Hound to NYC. The whole time while I was on the bus I was praying that no one would look at me and tell that I was running away. I had no ID and was hoping that I would be able to get away with it while in NY.

Q told me that he couldn't come with me because he had things to do in Greensboro. He instructed me that his son Larry would be picking me up from the bus station and that I was to make money and come back in about a week. Little did he know, I had no intentions on returning to Greensboro anytime soon and at that time how I was feeling, forever.

I was constantly thinking and called myself planning on how I would make a lot of money and eventually find a job and my own place to stay. I knew that NYC was huge and had a lot going on and believed that I wouldn't get caught by the police or any family. I had no ID and no real idea on what was to be expected. I just knew that I had to make it until my 18th birthday and if Q's son was anything like he was, I would have someone kindhearted and dumb enough to believe the lies that I had set forth to keep up until my birthday.

Little did I know, it was the exact opposite of what I had in my mind.

As soon as I stepped off the bus, I was overwhelmed with disappointment, fear, and a horrible odor. I had pictured NYC to be this beautiful place where the lights where bright and the people were smiling and happy.

Instead I was greeted by a raggedy bus terminal filled with homeless people and people from nationalities that I haven't even heard of all moving so fast and aggressive to wait on the same line as the person that they just almost trampled over. I quickly grabbed the prepaid cell phone that Q had bought me at Walmart and dialed his sons number. He told me that he was waiting for me at an intersection about two blocks away, and as soon as I came out of the terminal I was to make a right.

I got myself together and made sure I was portraying the exact opposite of how I was feeling. I wanted to come off as strong, sexy and tough. Not even realizing that I looked like a country bumpkin who was standing out to everyone in a horrible way. It was either me being scared or Mike gave me the wrong directions, but I found myself making a right turn but still ended up getting lost.

I counted the blocks as I crossed the small streets and just knew that it was two blocks. I called him, and he asked me where I was. Me being the smartass at the time told him I don't know I'm not from here duh. In return he asked me to look up at the street signs and read him the intersection. He seemed shocked and asked me how I got way over there and told me to turn around and walk around the corner. I did just that and could have sworn I was going the exact same way that I had come. Everything looked the same except for the people.

I called him again, and once again I was deemed lost. He asked me to read him the intersection again and stay right where I was. I stood on that corner so nervous for what seemed like forever! Everyone was rushing pass me as if I wasn't even standing there. Eventually a light skin guy with short hair and waves and a fresh pair of uptowns approached me and asked me what my name was. I told him D and he stated with a blank stare and without introducing himself,

"O ok come on, get in the car." Of course, saying the first thing that came to my mind, "That was rude like who are you?" Before I knew it, I was on the ground with a busted lip and him yelling at me, "Watch your fucking mouth, I'm not my father." My cheap clip-on ponytail was laying right next to me as I looked up with blood running down my mouth crying looking for someone to help me.

He started yelling again, "Get the fuck up and let's go. Nobody going to save you! People mind their business here. Welcome to NYC." I quickly grabbed my ponytail and bag and followed him to the car across the street where there where 3 other people inside. A guy who couldn't have been no older than me was driving which I learned later that his name was Ray. Another older guy in the front with a laptop in his lap named Omni and a younger light skin girl in the back seat who never said a peep the whole time that we were in the car. All looking either at their phones or straight ahead.

I was so scared and kept thinking to myself what the fuck did I get myself into. After what just happened I just knew that I was getting ready to be kidnaped, raped and probably killed. I just got in the car anyway and said to myself fuck it, if something does happen I'll go out fighting and I'm sure I won't be missed anyway.

I hurried up and got into the backseat of the car and sat in the middle. I was still thinking about what happened and my mind was racing a mile a minute. I had nowhere else to run to. No idea where I was other than me knowing I was in NYC. How was I going to clean the blood off my face? Was anyone in the car going to even mention the fact that I was almost covered in blood and what just happened? Is my lip swollen? Should I just get out the car and run? Before I could even figure out my next move, Larry asked me where the phone and money at that Q had given me. I quickly handed both over to Larry and afterwards he called Q and told him that I made it safe. I reached for the phone after hearing Q ask to speak to me. Larry then told Q as if I wasn't even sitting there,

"She don't want to talk to you right now. She said she's tired." I just sat that with my mouth wide open with the side eye. Larry hung up the phone after asking Q to email the nude pictures that he had taken of me while I was with him. A few minutes later Omni introduced himself to me as O. "You know anything about Craigslist?" I looked up at him, "No." "So all it is a website where you upload your pictures on and dates call you to either come to you or you go to them. How were you making money in NC?" "I was walking the streets." Everyone started laughing hard. I was confused. I didn't know that there was another way other than the streets except for the strip club and I knew I couldn't do that because I didn't know anyone who would let me inside with no ID. Omni looked in the back seat at Larry, "Yo where to?" Fifteen minutes later, I was in Brooklyn.

CONFESSION AND TIP NUMBER THREE:

WHILE HOEING IN NY, NEVER EVER FUCK ON TOP OF THE BLANKET OR EVEN THE BED AND ALWAYS WATCH OUT FOR BEDBUGS

On the way to Brooklyn I was so intrigued with the people, highways, bridges and all the tall buildings that we passed that I almost forgot that I had blood everywhere and that I was still in pain and shock about what just happened. It was so crowded and fast! Even in what was pointed out to me to be the projects, everyone was dressed impressively. Once we got across the Brooklyn Bridge, Larry begun to explain to me how to "answer the phone" when a date calls. "All you have to do is try to sound sexy and talk fast. Let them know that you are only doing outcalls for $160 hr. Let's do some test runs. Pick up the phone and act like I'm calling you."

By the end of the practice calls, Larry ended up calling me slow and told me I need to speed up and toughing up or someone was going to try to date me without giving me money. He also told me that once I go into a dates house I need to touch their dicks to make sure that they were not the police and to make sure that no one else was in the house. Once I get my money, count it and make sure it was real before I even take my clothes off. Afterwards, hold the money in one hand, and do what I had to do with the other one. He said that even though I tell them that I'll be there for an hour, I need to hurry up and let them cum only one time and that's it.

I had so many questions and so many things running through my mind but was to scared to ask. I just shook my head ok. The girl who was in the backseat finally looked up and asked Omni to take her home.

We drove to what was later known to me as Ocean Hill Projects. There were so many people outside and so much happening at once. Larry asked her "Yo, can she come upstairs with you and clean herself up a little bit." "Yea its cool. Come on." I looked at Larry and thought to myself I do not know this girl. Hell, I don't even know where I am! I just knew from the rap videos and the things that I see on TV that bad things happen in the projects in NY. She stepped out of the car and I followed right behind her. I thought, maybe I could get some information about what was going on with this whole craigslist thing and who the guys where to her since we would be alone.

We walked up to a building and headed straight for the elevator. While on the elevator she explained to me that her family was home and if they ask, I'm her friend from school. After she said that I looked closer at her and realized that she couldn't have been no more than 14 or 15. I was stunned as my head once again started spinning with questions and how's. But then I had to remember that where I came from we were doing similar things at her age just out in the streets.

As soon as she opened the door I was disgusted. The apartment was so nasty with roaches, leftover food, and everything just everywhere. There where was a crackhead nodding off on the couch that was worn down with stains everywhere. Two kids running around and loud music and weed smoke coming from a room near the back of the apartment.

She showed me where her bathroom was and told me that there should be paper towel somewhere in there where I could wipe my face off. I went in the bathroom and reached for the light switch and a roach jumped on my hand. I screamed and started shaking my hand. She looked at me like she was offended, "Don't tell me that your scared of roaches." I just looked at her and she started laughing, "O I forgot you are

from the south. Girl this the projects, everybody got roaches."
I couldn't have been so disgusted and couldn't wait until I left.

I walked into the bathroom to find used needles in the sink
and a tub filled with dirt and just nasty. The toilet had piss all
over it and I couldn't even bare to stand it. "Umm, I need to
get something out of the car, I'll be right back." I don't think
that I ever walked so fast in my life. I didn't even care that
people were staring at me.

I hurried my ass down the stairs and jumped back into the
car. Larry, Omni and Q were all looking at me and Larry
asked me what happened. "Her apartment was disgusting. Is
there a gas station or restaurant nearby?" They all started
busting out laughing for what seemed like forever. Omni
nodded his head to Ray "Yo go to the gas station around the
way."

I quickly ran inside and asked an Indian looking guy could
I use the restroom. He smiled asked me what happened and
started laughing. I looked at him and rolled my eyes as he
pointed me to the bathroom where I quickly washed my face
and changed my shirt. I walked back into the car and before I
could even sit-down, Larry was shoving the phone in my face
and telling me to answer it how I told you to.

I answered the phone and repeated what I had learned. "Ok
baby, text me your address and ill be on my way." As soon as
the phone hung up, I got call after call after call. I eventually

started sounding like a pro within a matter of minutes! Larry nudged me, "Look in the phone and give me the first address that you got." I gave him the address and he entered it into a GPS. We had just so happened to be about three minutes from the actual address.

Larry told me to text the date and let him know that I was on my way. I did just that and the date let me know that he'll be waiting for me downstairs and to make sure I was quiet and didn't slam the gate. We drove past the address and Omni pointed the house out to me. After we turned the corner, Larry gave me a condom and quickly reminded me that I had thirty minutes to make the date cum and make sure he was not the police and to get the money before I do anything. He also told me that if the date asked, to tell him that I had taken a taxi over there and my taxi was waiting for me outside, so I couldn't go over the time limit.

I got out the car hoping that I turned the right corner and didn't get lost. I found the address, opened the metal gate to the building and sure enough a man met me at the door. He appeared to be African. He had on no shirt with some swimming trunks and some flip flops. He ushered me into the front door with his hand signaling me to keep quiet. It smelled horrible inside. Like musk and stale meat.

We walked up one flight of stairs and he started taking his pants down right there in the hallway. After seeing half of the things that I had saw throughout the day I can honestly say that I was not shocked. I whispered, "Hey baby, you got the money for me?" I counted out $160 in all twenties, put the condom on him and proceeded to do what I was paid to. He was pleased after about four short minutes. He pulled his pants up and walked me to the door. Just like that, straight off the greyhound no sleep and a swollen lip, I was officially a hoe.

CONFESSION AND TIP NUMBER FOUR:

WHILE DOING OUTCALLS, MAKE SURE YOU CARRY PLENTY OF WET WIPES AND MOUTHWASH

For the next six hours or so it was pretty much the same thing. Back to back phone calls and dates. Some were good, and others were better. Around 7am when the phone finally slowed down, Larry had instructed Ray to drive us to a local roach motel in Hempstead Long Island called the Curtsey Hotel. It was a rundown hotel and you could smell the sex and mold as soon as you walked in the lobby. I hadn't been in too many hotels in my life, but I was sure that bad things happened at this one and pretty much after the last 48 hours that I have had, I really didn't care how this hotel looked. I just wanted to take a nice hot shower and lay down.

After Larry said his goodbyes to Omni and Ray, he told me to quickly grab my bag out the trunk and meet him in the lobby. We checked in and got on the pissy smelling elevator to go up to our room. As soon as we stepped into the room I snatched my ponytail off, undressed and showered.

I was in pain all over my body. I appreciated the long hot shower. It gave me some time to reflect on everything that has happened to me within the last couple of days. Not only that, I felt so disgusted and tried my best to wash off every trick that I had had that night. I knew that I would be doing this for a while until I got on my feet, so I was trying to figure out ways to numb all the pain physically and mentally. Something had to make this seem ok to me.

The bright side to all of this was that I had made over $1200 in a couple of hours. I figured this was an amazing start. I could use this money to pay for a hotel for about a week and treat myself to my hair and nails, and a few outfits to make myself look more appealing. I just needed to sit and generate a plan and hopefully Larry could help me with all of this. Once again, I was wrong.

As soon as I stepped out of the shower I proceeded to lotion my body and prepare to get some sleep. Larry was sitting in the corner of the room rolling up a blunt. I reached into my bag to count all the money that I had made, and it was gone. I looked up at Larry, "Yo did I just so happen drop money on the floor in here?" He started laughing and I couldn't seem to figure out what he was laughing. "You know damn well all that money is in my pocket where it belongs."

I was confused, and I am sure it showed on my face because he quickly followed up by asking me if I had ever had a pimp. "Look, I know my father is soft and wasn't doing what he was supposed to be doing with you." I was still confused and cut him off "Can I just have my money please? I have plans with this money and I am tired, and I really don't need any more drama today." "O yea? What plans do you have." "Honestly, I plan on getting a hotel room and getting my hair and nails done so I could find some more work. I also need to save up and find somewhere to permanently lay my head."

Without even looking up from rolling his blunt, "O you have goals. That's a good thing. At least you're not stupid and want something to have for yourself. I can help you get to where you need to go. Don't worry you're in good hands. You don't want to just leave your money lying around for somebody to rob you. I'll hold on to your money for now and start saving it up for you. But on another note, get dressed. We are about to start crossing off some of these goals. Let's go get your hair and shit done."

I was way too worn out to even second guess anything that he had said or question him any further. "O, by the way you'll be taking the night off, so you can get some sleep." I threw on some sweat pants, a t-shirt and wrapped my hair in a scarf. After he smoked his blunt, we talked a little more and he seemed a little nicer than when I first met him. Afterwards, we walked downstairs and got a taxi from in front of the hotel and proceeded to go to what would eventually become my second home, Jamaica Ave.

We stopped on 165th street, what I like to call the brick road. I was once again shocked at all the different type of people and the loud reggae music I was hearing. It was all types of things going on.

People walking down the street selling stuff, different smells of food, clothing stores everywhere and of course bums. We walked down the brick road and stopped in front of a nail salon and Larry gave me $100 and told me to get my nails and feet done. He then asked me what size I wore so he can go and get me a few outfits and some underclothes and a pair of shoes.

I couldn't help but to fall asleep while I was getting my nails and feet done. My brain and body could no longer take it. I just knew that when I woke up, my nails looked like I was a hand model in a magazine. They were so perfect and unlike anything I had ever seen before.

Larry came back inside the nail salon just as I was finishing. He had lots of bags with him and asked me if I was ready to go. We left the nail salon and he told me that he had bought a few nice wigs so that I wouldn't have to go and get my hair done and I could go and catch up on some sleep. We stopped at a Jamaican restaurant around the corner from where I had gotten my nails done and sat and ate.

I was curious because I had never seen or heard of some of the things that were on the menu. I've had plenty of beef patties and curry chicken, so I settled on what I knew best and ordered that. We got our food and Larry hailed a taxi. He told me that he had some errands to run and that he would meet me back at the hotel later tonight. He gave me $100 and told me to hold on to that for pocket money in case I wake up and wanted to go and get something to eat and to pay for the taxi. He told the taxi driver to drop him off at Baisley projects and take me back to the hotel.

As soon as I got back into my hotel room I looked at the clothes and shoes that Larry had picked out. I was impressed. Most of the clothes where pink or some shade of pink. I also had a pair of pink pumps and a pair of pink sandals and a bag that matched perfectly with them both and about five matching bra and panty sets. I also had a long wig with a bang that looked good on me. It had the perfect cut bangs that highlighted my big bright eyes and stopped just below my bra.

I had noticed that he bought some make up for me to use as well.

I'm thinking to myself, I could really trust him. After I ate my food I took another shower, put my phone on the charger and hit the bed so hard I almost missed it.

I ended up sleeping all the way until about 3am and woke up to my phone ringing off the hook. I called Larry a few times and he didn't answer, and I had started to wonder if he was really coming back. I began to panic. I had no idea what I was going to do or where I was going to go if he didn't. My mind started going into hustler mode. All I kept thinking was that I could answer my phone and make some more money just in case he didn't come back. That way I can at least pay for the hotel room again until I figure out what to do.

I was pissed, because he had the rest of my money with him that I had made the previous night, but I couldn't dwell on that. He had mentioned to me about in calls, meaning that the dates would come to me. So, I called back the last three numbers who had called me and gave them my price and the address to the hotel that I was in. I hopped in the shower and put on one of the bra and panty sets that Larry had picked out earlier that hid my gut and highlighted my 5'7, thick chocolate figure and 38 DD breast. I brushed my hair back and put the long wig on with some eyeliner and mascara.

Three hours later, I had $400 in my pocket and had talked my last date into putting the room in his name. I knew I couldn't do it because I had no ID. He obliged, and I paid for another night.

Once he left I started calling and texting Larry to see where he was and if he could bring me my money. He never answered and I began to panic again.

I was hungry and needed time to think so I walked outside and crossed the street and went to a little store that I had peeped earlier. While I was standing in line I got another call. I thought why not, I could use all the money I can get right now, and It ended up being Omni on the other end of the phone. "Hello." "Yo shorty I got some bad news. Larry got bit last night." "Bit by what? Did he die?" Omni let out a aggravated sigh, "No not bit like that damn! He got arrested ma. But look, I will be at the hotel a little later on to pick you up so we can talk." "But he has all my money? He just left me out …" "Look don't worry about none of that. You're going to be in good hands until he comes home. Just hold on to any money you got on you because your going to need it later to post online and to pay the driver to drive you around like we did the other night. O and make sure you dress nice. Its Friday and we are going to Manhattan."

I was relieved. I thought that I was left for dead. I grabbed a sandwich and some snacks and went back to my hotel room. Around 7pm, I started getting dressed and made sure my hair, make up and outfit was on point. Around 8:30 Omni called me and told me that he was waiting for me downstairs. I stashed my money in my bag, grabbed my phone charger and was out the door looking like a brand-new person.

As soon as I had gotten in the car, Omni and Ray both said at the same time "Damn!" Omni asked me jokingly, "What happened to the girl from the other day." "Larry took me shopping and picked out all of this." "You look good ma those bangs are a good look for you. I see your swelling done went down to. But anyway, are you ready to get to work?" All I could think about was bettering my situation and without hesitation, I shook my head yes and smiled.

On the way to Manhattan Omni repeated the same thing that he did when I met him. He would be posting my pictures online and he also asked me if I had remembered how to answer the phone. I told him I had taken some calls earlier because I thought I was going to be stranded. That was a big mistake.

He smiled, rubbing his hands together, "O Yea, how much did you make?" "O only about $400." "Ok, ok, not bad. I see your having some beginners luck. How much do you got on you? Give me $60 so I can get you posted and pay the driver." I reached in my bag and handed over what was requested while sitting in the back seat hyping myself up about my night. I was hoping that I could make at least another $600 so that I could try and start to look for an apartment. Reflecting, I had no idea how I was going to achieve all these things without no ID at 17 years old. I had made it this far, so I figured that I would cross that bridge once get to it.

The night kicked off with me having a date near second avenue with a guy who I would later become great friends with. He was my first regular. His name was Marc and he was one of those white guys who smoked lots of weed. He lived in a four story walk up and by the time I reached his apartment I was out of breath and tired. He must have known that I would be because he greeted me with a smile, kiss on the cheek and a cold bottle of water.

"Hello beautiful. I know it's a lot of stairs. How are you feeling?" While trying to catch my breath, I replied, "I'm doing good baby, how are you? Thank you for the water." The inside of his apartment made me lose the rest of the little bit of breath that I had inside of me. It was huge and had been decked out in all white. I had never seen anything like this before.

"Catch your breath, take your shoes off and meet me on the sofa." Did he just say sofa? I did just that and removed my clothes and sat right beside him. I had to remember that I was there on business, so I tried to seduce him and signaled him to give me the money.

"Ok so here's the deal. I want you all night. I like you and I know I'm going to have a lot of fun with you. Can you stay until about 5 am? How's $1000.?" I thought he was playing and knew that I was being punked until he counted out ten one hundred-dollar bills and sat them next to me while I stared at him with my mouth wide open. I had heard about things like this happening to people but for some reason I couldn't believe that it was happening to me.

He told me that there was no rush and that he wanted to sit and talk for a while. He gave me a glass of wine and we sat on his couch and talked a little bit about everything from, TV shows to the local news for about an hour. My phone started ringing off the hook and I excused myself and saw that it was Omni making sure that I was ok. I text him back and let him know that I had been payed to stay there until 5am and to come back and pick me up then.

I went back into the living room with Marc and out of nowhere he began to kiss me. He then took all my clothes off slowly and laid me down on the all-white mink carpet on his living room floor followed by the best head I have ever gotten my whole 17 years of living on this earth. After he slipped on a condom, Marc had me twisted and turned in all types of positions. I had never had anyone be that passionate and generous with me.

After a long night of passion I felt refreshed once he woke me up around 4. We both were smiling, and he had the shower water running and waiting for me. As I wrapped up my shower and got dressed I received a text message from Omni that let me know that he was waiting for me downstairs. I said my goodbyes and thank you's to Marc and he had let me know that he would call me again soon and to save his number.

I couldn't wait to get back into the car and tell Omni and Ray what just happened. I couldn't believe it. As soon as I got back in the car Omni started busting out laughing and joking with me asking if I had a good time. "Yes. I did." From the smile on your face, I can tell." could tell. Let me get $60 dollars for the driver. The phone should still be ringing do you want to work some more or get dropped off to the hotel." "O nah, I'm taking it in." "Aight bet. I'm going to come upstairs with you though, so we can talk."

Ray dropped us both off at my hotel and as soon as I got inside the room I had snatched my wig off and once again hit the bed. Omni looked at me and smiled while sitting on the edge of the bed rolling a blunt. "Yea I know your tired. On another note, I know someone with a room for rent and you can move in today if you want. Its clean and its low key. Larry had mentioned to me about your little goals and I can help you way better than anyone else."

I couldn't believe the good luck that I was having. I explained to him that I didn't have an ID and gave him a small detail about what went down in NC. "Girl don't worry about that. That's normal in these streets. This is NY. Money talks ma."

He moved closer and stood up and gave me a long hug that felt warm and inviting and ended up kissing me. I was caught off guard, thinking in my head "O god he wants to have sex with me." Why not. He was getting ready to move me into a private room with my own bathroom. I could get out of this roach motel and finally start really saving my money.

Looking into my eyes while holding me by my waist, he also told me that he could help me get into a strip club not too far from where I would be staying. That way I didn't have to sleep with all these different men and still make money. He began to undress me and before I knew it I was getting what felt at the time to be the best sex in the world.

He was talking to me as he was fucking me in every position imaginable. It was rough, but I liked it. Afterwards he held me and started whispering to me. He then asked me a question that I had no idea would make my life even worse than it already was. "So, you want me to be your new daddy?" I had no idea about the deal that I was making with the devil himself. But I had just been fucked so good, I quietly answered yes and fell peacefully asleep.

CONFESSION AND TIP NUMBER FIVE:

NEVER TRUST A PIMP THAT LIVES WITH HIS MOMMA

I woke up the next day with my head laying on Omni's chest and noticed that he was staring at me smiling. I've never been a morning person, so I couldn't even process half of what was going on. All I had known is that I felt amazing. I felt as if though a ton of weight had been lifted off my shoulders. I was finally accomplishing some type of goals and felt as if though I didn't run away for no reason and I was proving everyone wrong.

After Omni and I showered, he instructed me to get dressed and pack my things, so we could head to my new place. Once

I was packed, we headed downstairs and met Ray in front of the hotel and I didn't even bother to look back.

Twenty minutes later we arrived in a beautiful neighborhood known as Cambria Heights. It was filled with short blocks that hosted one and two-family homes with yards and drive ways. I felt like I wasn't even in NYC anymore. It was a far stretch from what I had seen so far.

My land lord was waiting for us at the beginning of the drive way. He was a West Indian man who was married with two kids. He ushered Omni and I into the home and we walked downstairs into a finished off basement that looked like a small one-bedroom apartment. It was fully furnished with a small kitchen and a full bathroom. It was clean quiet and peaceful. Exactly what I had needed.

My land lord opened a door to a small furnished room and quickly went over his house rules. I was nervous and praying to god that he didn't ask me for ID or anything about my personal life. He told me that the whole basement was mine and that I could come and go as I please. Don't smoke, pay rent on time and I had nothing to worry about.

He gave me my keys and told me to store his number in my phone and I smiled inside knowing that I was 17 years old with my own place. I had been through hell the last two weeks, but it was worth going through to be at this point now.

After I had put my little bit of things away Omni sat next to me on my new bed and we began to have a conversation.

"You know you're in good hands, right? I'm going to make sure your token care of. You don't have anything to worry about. I know that you are running from something in NC, but you don't have to worry about any of that anymore. You're my bitch now so your good. Got it." I was still a little confused with all of this, but I was so happy, and I sat there and listened.

"There is so much more to this game that you need to know. Eventually, you're going to have wife n laws so don't get to comfortable with living on your own." I was curious, and felt like I could ask him anything, so I did. 'What's a wife n law?" Laughing, he responded "I'm a pimp and I'm your daddy. You will have other girls that work with you and for me and we will all work together as a team and grow. I don't like the term hoes. We are more like a family who makes money together and take care of each other no matter what happen."

Without reading the fine print, I was sold at family. That's something that I haven't really known. I figured hell, I had a decent place to rest my head and someone to help me stack my paper and get to know NYC, I could meet him half way. Plus, I didn't want to lose everything he had help me to get so far. "Any more questions? I need to go home and do somethings before we go to work. It's a Tuesday night, so it's going to be slow. You can wear jeans and a t shirt and be fine."

Omni stood up gave me money and told me to walk around a little to get to know my new neighborhood. There where stores on almost every corner and plenty of restaurants that delivered. I hugged him good bye and anxiously freshened up, so I could go and learn my new neighborhood. I walked around for about thirty minutes before I grabbed a Beef Pattie and some snacks and drinks to keep in my new apartment. I figured I would go grocery shopping later once I made some more money and got settled in. I took a hot shower and decided on taking a nap before I hit the trap later.

I woke up to a slow moist kiss from Omni. I was confused and shocked that he would even kiss me knowing what I do with my mouth for money. He must have really liked me and was happy that I decided to be his. I already knew what time it was, so I just stretched, smiled and proceeded with my new routine. Shit, shave, shower and makeup. I grabbed some condoms and my phone and followed him into the car where Ray was waiting for us as usual. I had concluded that he would be my permanent driver and as soon as the thought crossed my mind, "Yo get use to Ray. Make sure you save his number in your phone just in case I'm not around and you need to go somewhere."

"Ok I'll save it now. Where are we working at tonight? After the magical night that I had in Manhattan I want to go back there." That's when he took my life from worst to horrible. "O nah ma, I got something else in mind for us tonight. Don't get nervous though it's basically the same thing that you were doing down in NC. It's Tuesday, so you not going to make any money on the phone. We call it the blade up here and we were going to start with Something Blvd."

I kept repeating "Something Blvd?" and him and Ray started busting out laughing. Omni explained that its "Sutphin Blvd", not 'Something Blvd.' I felt stupid as I laughed out loud. I figured if I could handle the streets in Greensboro and make over $600 in two hours I should be good here in NY.

We pulled up to the corner of Sutphin and South Rd. The neighborhood seemed rowdy and I could tell that I was in the hood. "All you have to do is walk up and down the street and if a car pulls over you know what to do. But look, this isn't the south, need to walk a little faster than how you have been. You're going to be fine. I'll be near you at all times, call me every time you finish a date, so you can break. If I don't pick up the phone, just come back to this corner."

I was kind of nervous, but I knew that I had money to make. I got out the car and begun my journey. I took some deep breaths and hit my best hoe walk. It seemed like no one was outside, but the energy was high as if I was surrounded by people. I noticed a few crackheads and occasionally some more girls who I figured where doing the same thing that I was. But they were walking faster than I was with their heads down.

I knew better than to stop and talk to them. I learned from spending most of my summers in the North to mind your business and don't speak even if you are spoken to. I reached the block of 113th and Sutphin Blvd as a green minivan slowly came to a stop. There was a small white puppy hanging out of the window with a young light skin guy driving. I approached the car, "Hey baby what you need?" "Half and half but I only got $100 on me." I was thirsty to catch a date and sit down so I took it and told him he had fifteen minutes.

We drove to the back of some brick buildings that looked like the projects that Omni was from behind some dumpsters. I smiled, "So what's your name hand..." before I could get out the rest of my sentence I was punched in my left eye. I instantly felt dizzy as I tried to figure out what was going on. I didn't even have a chance to catch my breath and react before my leggings had been ripped off and I felt him bending me over the seat while shoving his dick straight into my ass. All I could do was scream at the pain as I felt blood dripping down my leg while my heart beat grew faster and faster in panic. I just knew that after he was done raping me, he was going to kill me and leave me inside of the dumpster that we were behind. He punched me hard on the side of my stomach and began to choke me, "Shut the fuck up. I swear to God if you don't shut the fuck up I'm going to slice your fucking throat." I just cried as I lay there bent over the back seat of a minivan with a dog staring at me while I was being raped in the back of the projects.

Believe it or not I started to pray and ask God to please not let me die this way. I felt my eye swelling as it began to close. After a few more seconds he finally stopped ,"Get on your knees and open your fucking mouth." and he shoved his dick to the back of my throat and nutted. He then covered my mouth and told me to swallow it or he would kill me. I did as he said. He then ripped the remainder of my clothes off and told me to take off my shoes and get the fuck out of his car.

He opened the door pushed me out and pulled off as I sat there naked on the cold ground with nothing but a bra on. I had no idea what to do but luckily for me I was alive, and I still had my cell phone stashed under my bra. Shaking and scared that he would change his mind and come back to kill me, I called Omni.

"Omni, please come get me this guy just raped me…" "Yo where you at. I know your scared, but I don't know where you at so walk to the nearest intersection and tell me where you at." I was screaming and yelling and crying and asking did he not just hear me tell him that I was naked. Omni yelled at me, "I don't care about none of that. Do you want me to come get you or not?" I sat behind that dumpster in shock but quickly got up and walked to the nearest corner.

I had seen a sign that said Jamaica Houses and read him the address that was below the sign. Two minutes later I saw Ray and I couldn't have been happier. Omni got out of the car, looked at me, and started to hug me as he ushered me into the backseat of the car. Omni "What happened to you?" I couldn't even explain. I just cried. I cried so hard I began to get a headache.

I eventually mustered up the courage to tell him that I just wanted to go home and twenty minutes later we were walking down the stairs to enter my apartment. Omni ran me a hot bath and brought me a towel with ice inside of it. I was hurt. Mentally and Physically. I didn't know if I should call the police or go to the hospital. What made It even worst was that the next thing that came out of Omnis mouth was just as heartbreaking as what just happened to me.

"Hurry and get showered and redressed. I'll be waiting for you outside." I just sat there stunned, shocked, embarrassed and just once again confused. I had just gotten raped and was scared for my life. My thoughts where running a mile a minute and I felt as if though I was going to pass out. I was thinking a mixture of things. Did I catch an STD? Where was the blood coming from? Omnis not protecting me or doing anything about it? Should I go to the hospital? Did he just tell me to get dressed? I looked at him and yelled to the top of my lungs, "Are you fucking kidding me! I just got raped and almost killed! I have a black eye and your telling me to get dressed to go back into the streets?"

I continued to cry as he looked at me. He started to walk towards me and I was expecting him to give me a hug and tell me that everything was going to be ok and that I was right. But instead I was met with a kick on the same side of my stomach that I had just been punched on. Crying I laid there in pain and disbelief. Everything just hit me at once and it felt as if though I was chocking. Omni began to choke me

"Once again, get up and get dressed so you can get my money." He stood there and before he had a chance to hit me again I got up showered and got dressed. While we were in the car, I sat in the backseat in a blur to afraid to cry. We pulled back up to Sutphin and South Road. Before I got out the car Omni instructed me to start screening my dates and to only take older dates. It was my fault and I should have known better than to get in the car with a young guy.

I got out of the car and once again begun my journey. This time with a swollen eye and what felt like a bruised rib. There where way more girls out this time. I just followed suit and walked with my head down to the car that had slowed down and turned the corner right next to where I was standing. I asked the usual questions, got in and was thankful that he pulled right over not too far from where I got in at. He gave me the requested money and I begin to service him the best was that I could despite the pain that I was in.

For the next two weeks Omni made me work on Sutphin. He told me that I couldn't take any calls until I healed because the dates would turn me away. He started to get meaner and meaner as the days went by. I was to be scared and still so confused to even question him. I was only allowed to catch a minimum of three dates per night and I was barely eating. There were even a few days where Omni forgot to give me money for food and drinks and I other days I was way too tired to even walk to the store to get food. My eye eventually healed, and the pain had eased in my side. I had started to lose weight and the clothes that Larry had bought when I first got into NY where falling off me.

I eventually started to think how I was going to get myself out of this situation. I couldn't go back home because I would just end up in prison because of my charges and I couldn't run away from Omni because I didn't know anyone else in NY that could help me. I was stuck. Hoping and praying for a way out.

It was a Friday night and Omni had once again woken me up telling me to get dressed but make sure my hair and makeup was on point and to make sure I was wearing heels. Omni had bought me some new dresses and wigs to where while I worked so I was looking up to part. I went through my usual routine and met Omni and Ray outside. We parked at our usual location and I began my routine journey.

I was hoping to have and early night because my feet were hurting from the slow and long Thursday night. I saw a gold Maxima slowly turn the corner next to where I was standing. I walked up to the driver side and was met with an older gentleman that was fly in Yankee fitted and an all-white velour sweat suit. He had to be about 50 years old and I figured he should be easy and quick. I asked him what he needed, and he followed my question with one simple word………. "You!"

CONFESSION AND TIP NUMBER SIX:

MAKE A NAME FOR YOURSELF BY BENDING AT THE WAIST AND NOT AT THE KNEE

At the time, I had no idea about the certain questions that you were supposed to ask before getting in a car with a date so of course with me being green, I had no idea that I just got into a car with an old school pimp by the name of Halo. As soon as I sat inside of his car he asked me what my name is. I smiled and told him Dee. He smiled with his smooth deep voice, "Dee? What kind of name is that for a hoe? Your new name is Joy because your beautiful smile can bring joy to anyone."

I just sat there too dumb to even question why he was giving me a nickname and even dumber to realize that we had just gotten on a highway. As soon as I realized that I was a little further than I had intended to be, I asked "So are we going to a specific hotel that you know about?" "We were going to my house. It's only about 20 min from where we at right now. It's in Brooklyn." "Ok that's cool just as long as you are comfortable with bringing me back once we were done." He agreed but added only if I wanted to. I just looked at him a smiled as I relaxed with my head back listening to the old school hip hop blaring through his speakers.

We pulled up to a three-family brick building and he put his car in park. He smiled at me once again before he started questioning me. "How old are you? Where are you from because you're not from here sounding like you've been a farmer your whole life." I couldn't help but to bust out laughing. I had to had laughed for about a whole two minutes as he just sat there and starred at me.

Once I calmed down and he pulled his seat back and put both of his hands behind his head. I took this as a signal that he was ready for me to do what I do. Rubbing my hands on his jeans "So do you want just head?" He smiled "No. I told you what I want. I want you." "Lol. I know that but give me $100 so I can go ahead and please you." He just sat there and smiled even harder showing all his gold teeth "You know I'm a pimp right Joy?"

I shook my head as my heart fell to my feet. I got so nervous as I imagined the ass whooping that Omni was going to give me for talking to another pimp. I hoped that because Halo was older he wouldn't be as mean, and I could easily try and talk my way into him just dropping me off. Halo put his hand on my shoulder and told me to relax, "I already know about that bumb ass fake ass simp Omni and it would be nothing for me to call him and let him know that you won't be returning. I know how grimy he is, and I heard all about what happened to you a few weeks ago behind the forties. You see Joy if you choose me, you wouldn't have to worry about being treated like any less than you deserve. A real pimp doesn't have to put his hands on his women. All it takes is a solid team to make sure we all get to the top. Before you even decide, come see how I am living and meet your wife n laws."

At this point I was thinking and asking was this my way out from Omni? What happens if Halo was telling the truth about the game that he was spitting? I mean what exactly did I have to lose? Halo then got out of his car and walked around the car and opened the car door for me. We then walked to the front door of his building and briefly down a short hall. He opened his door and I was amazed at the black and red décor of his 4-bedroom apartment. "Joy give me your phone, have a seat and I will be right back."

I didn't care or even bother to ask him why. It was dead and probably filled with death threats from Omni. The front door opened, and two teenage boys who couldn't have been no older than 15 walked in both wearing Nike sweat suits and Timbs. They both looked at me smiled, "O shit! Pops got a bad little chocolate thing on his hands. What's your name?" I was scared and once again thinking I was lied to and that I was about to be raped again and started to panic.

Halo came back down the hall accompanied by an older dark skin lady named Cola and a Spanish girl who looked to be around the same age as I was with red hair named Amazing. Halo started playfully fighting with the two boys and I then learned that those where him and Colas sons. He introduced everyone in the room to me and told them that I would be joining their family.

I just sat there amazed at everything that I was seeing and wondering if those were really his sons and if so how are the all managing to live together with hoes. Cola came and sat beside me smiling and reached and gave me a long hug. "Hey Joy welcome to the family. I'm bottom, and we are going to take good care of you here." I had been told about a bottom before and had known from her age and the ease that she was in that she had to be a pro at this point. She told her sons to go to their room and get their homework done and rolled a blunt briefly after. Halo and Amazing sat on the couch across from us. Amazing seemed like she had an attitude and proved it by looking at halo and saying loudly while rolling her eyes, "She not gone last long, and she looks mad young. Have you looked at her ID?"

Halo laughed at her before telling her, "Stop starting shit and give her a chance. She just might last longer than you have the last two times that you have been here with your choosy ass." Cola busted out laughing and told me that she was choosy.

She's been coming and going with them for the past two years. Cola looked at me with a blank stare, "Don't let this bitch intimidate you. She just acting light skin. You are going to be ok here. Are you hungry? You want anything to drink?" I blushed and shook my head yes. "I'm glad you're not one of those shy girls scared to eat. We were just about to order Chinese."

Before she could even ask me, I had already told her that I wanted fried chicken wings with broccoli and garlic sauce. Amazing picked up her cell and ordered the food. Cola then asked me, "What size do you were in bra and panties and stilettos?" "I wear a 38DD in bra, size 12 in jeans and a size 10 I shoes." She got up, passed her blunt to Amazing, went down the hallway and came back with a handful of clothes and a pair of Hot Pink stilettos and placed them down on the black leather sofa beside me.

"You know how to dance right? We dance in this house girl. We don't walk the streets and we damn sure don't work the internet. That shit is to dangerous and you can get killed or locked up to damn fast." Sounds like my type of family.

Halo got up and signaled for me to follow him as he showed me around his apartment. His boys shared a room, with me and Amazing in the room right across the hall from theirs. Him and Cola slept in the back and there was another small room with a pole and gym equipment right next to theirs. "We work out every day in this house and I expect for you to learn some pole tricks, so you can make some good money in these clubs." I blushed with embarrassment. I couldn't even imagine me hanging from a pole at my weight. Halo must have been reading my mind because he told me don't worry about your weight. "Once you start working you're going to drop weight and tone up fast."

Halo escorted me back to the living room and gave each one of us a kiss before telling us that he was going to sleep, and he would see us when we got back from work the next morning. I started thinking how was we going to get to work? Who was going to watch us? I had so many questions and felt as if though I could ask. I turned and faced Cola "How are we getting to work, and I have danced before but not as a stripper." Amazing added her two cents, "Wow, I knew this bitch was green looking all goofy and smiling at everything and shit." Cola looked at her yelling, "Shut the fuck up, I bet she will run circles around your non-rhythm having ass. What the fuck is wrong with you? Take your shit and go in your room being all negative."

I was surprised to see Amazing doing as she was told. "She thinks she the shit because she's mixed but that bitch aint shit. The only reason she's still here is because Halo feels sorry for her dumb ass. Don't worry about her. She will come around. In the meantime, eat your food and get some rest. I'll give you a dress and some sandals to put on later. You can sleep right here on the couch since Amazing acting dumb. Make yourself comfortable and Ill teach you the ins and outs of the strip club once we get there. That way you don't freeze up. Like I told you earlier don't worry we got you covered."

Cola grabbed a blanket and towel and wash cloth, with a long t shirt that I knew was meaning for me to sleep in out of a small closet and placed it on the couch. She told me she would wake me up and headed into her room. I decided to take a hot shower and then ate my food. I laid on the couch with thoughts once again racing through my head. Not only was I running from NC, I was now running from Omni. What would happen if he found me? I took a deep breath and relaxed my mind and finally after telling myself repeatedly that I would be ok, and I fell asleep.

Around 11:30pm, Cola was tapping me on my shoulder waking me up. I'm surprised that I wasn't up already. Music was loud and blunts was being passed around. I already knew what time it was, so I gathered what I would be wearing to the club and packed a small bag with two dance outfits and the stilettos that Cola had given to me.

My stomach was in knots just thinking about Omni and what was ahead for me that night. Cola gave me a razor and told me to make sure that I shave everything. Once I was showered and dressed, I did my hair and makeup and we were out the door.

Cola drove us to an underground bar in downtown Brooklyn. It didn't seem as if there were to many people there at the time. Once again, she read my mind "I know it looks dead but it's still early and people will come around 2. They don't close until 4am so we got plenty of time to talk and I can show you a few things." Once we were at the door the bouncer asked for our ID's. Cola playfully punched him in the chest and told him that I was with them and there aren't any problems. The bouncer laughed "I know I know I was just playing with you OG Cola."

He then opened the door and I followed Cola and Amazing into a large room with a pole in the corner. It was dark and filled with the smell of weed and sex. We then went inside another room where there were two full length mirrors and about 4 other girls. Two were plus size and the other two were slim and dark skin. I followed Cola and Amazing into a corner as they started taking things out of there bag.

I watched all the girls carefully, studying their movements and what they were doing so I wouldn't have to ask to many questions. Cola instructed me to put on a pink thong one piece that tied at the waist that she had provided for me earlier. Amazing wore a bright red with red glitter makeup and red stiletto boots. I thought she looked so pretty. She had her hair swept up in a high bun and had even put in grey contacts. I smiled and told her, "Wow! You look amazing!" She laughed "I know that's my name bitch!" She had seemed to be in a better mood from earlier. Maybe she just needed some sleep. Cola looked just as good in an all-black one piece and white stilettos. These girls were pros and I knew I could learn a lot from them.

Cola started talking to me in a low tone whispering in my ear, "First don't smile too much. Don't talk to any young guys and don't be friendly with any of the other girls. If they start asking you questions tell them to ask me and I'll tell them. Basically, all your doing is walking up to a guy, gently touch his dick and ask him if he want a dance. Dances are $10 a song and if he wants a VIP its $125 for fifteen minutes. You keep $100 and then give the bouncer $25. Make sure you clean up and get the condom before you leave out of VIP and the only thing you are to do is give head. NO FUCKING." I just shook my head and followed suit. It sounded easy enough to me.

Cola handed me a red bull and told me to drink the rest for energy. I sat there sipping the red bull as we all started whispering about how raggedy the other girls looked. It was one girl who had on cheap lingerie and a stiff wig. Cola just looked at her and started laughing so hard it caused a chain reaction from me and Amazing once we peeped what she was laughing at. I was laughing so hard I felt like I had to poop. Matter of fact I did. I was embarrassed to tell Cola to show me the bathroom because who wants someone dancing on them in a thong after they have taken a poop.

"Yo Cola I think I gotta shit. Where's the bathroom?" "Girl its cool! We all do it and I came well prepared." She grabbed a smaller bag out of her bag that had a bar of soap and a few wash cloths and walked me to the bathroom which was on the other side of the dressing room. After she closed the door, she told me to spread my cheeks apart as far as I could before I sat down. As soon as I sat on the toilet the poop just came out so fast and hard as if it came out all at one time. For some reason I couldn't stop laughing and had even felt a little high.

I'm thinking to myself that I must have caught a contact from all the weed that was being smoked. I looked over at Cola and she was dancing in the mirror feeling on herself slowly while popping her gum super hard. I felt as if though I was moving in slow motion as I reached for the toilet paper. I stood up the best way I could and when I finally did start moving I felt so good! I just felt warm and cool at the same time and all I wanted to do was dance to the music that was playing.

Cola looked at me as I was wiping myself up with the soap and wash cloth. "At least you have rhythm lol! Are you nervous?" Feeling on my titties, "No. I feel good!" She smiled, "Good. Just remember what I told you." Once we were back inside the dressing room I had noticed a few more girls had arrived and Amazing had stepped on the floor. I wasn't paying much attention to anyone or anything else. I just knew that I could not stop licking my lips and dancing. She asked me if I was ready and I was.

A soon as I stepped on the floor an older Spanish guy grabbed me and shoved a $20 bill in my hand. I couldn't believe how sexy and confident I had felt while I was grinding and bending over on him. I looked up and had seen Amazing hanging upside down on the pole in the corner of the room and Cola was laughing and talking to the bouncer who had let us in earlier.

The Spanish guy started feeling on my boobs and out of nowhere I started talking nasty to him telling him he should take me to VIP, so I could make him feel special. He asked me how much and I told him $125. He said ok and reached inside of his pocket and gave me $140 in 20's. I escorted him to the small room that was designated for VIP. I gave the bouncer $40 and he gave me $15 back and I slid it inside of the small money bag that Cola let me borrow. Once we stepped inside the VIP room I immediately pulled out a condom and pulled down his pants. I was so horny and ready to please him. I anxiously put the condom on him and it seemed as if though he ejaculated within two minutes. He stood me up and tried to kiss me, but I dubbed it.

I wrapped the used condom inside of a baby wipe and took it with me in the dressing room. I still was dancing and bopping as I wiped my self off with a baby wipe and gargled some mouth wash. Cola came inside the dressing room hugging me and yelling, "Go bitch! That's what's up! You haven't been for thirty minutes and already catching fucking VIP's. I knew I was going to like you! Keep it up wifey." She told me to freshen up and put some gum in my mouth and gloss my lips before I walked back onto the floor.

I stepped back onto the floor and just that fast it was crowded. I danced my way over to a guy that was standing in the corner with a beer in his hand. I started grinding on him as he was placing numerous bills inside of my outfit. He asked me my name and we started to have a small conversation. "My name is Joy baby what's yours?" We talked for about ten minutes and then he popped the magic question. Another VIP! Go me! The rest of the night was pretty much the same thing. I was busting dance moves that I didn't even I had. Splits, heel stretches and all. By the time 3:30 am I had made about $500 and I wasn't outside or didn't have to have sex for it. We all got dressed and once we were inside the car Cola and Amazing were both praising me.

"I couldn't even tell that you never danced before. You did good Joy!" Amazing laughed and told Cola, "That wasn't nothing but that damn e and red bull that had her ass moving like that all night." By that time, I was tired and worn out and had heard her clear. Cola had given me a damn E pill and I didn't even know! I just stared at Cola with disbelief. "Joy did you die, and did you make money? Answer me when I'm talking to you girl." The tone of her voice had gone from sweet to serious and I just answered with anger, "No I didn't die but you didn't have to do that. I would have been straight regardless. I know how to make money." "Bitch please! You were nervous and shaking and shit. I had to give you something to calm you down and get you focused or you would have gotten scared." I felt a strong headache coming on and I didn't even bother to say another word. Cola asked for me and Amazing's money bags and put them both inside of her own. I just sat in the back seat smoking my cigarette and thinking to myself NYC aint shit.

CONFESSION AND TIP NUMBER SEVEN:
USE BITCH PLEASE WITH CAUTION

The next day I woke up with a headache and a sore body. I looked over to find Amazing lying next to me snoring. I gathered my things to take a hot shower and hopefully find some Tylenol or pain killers for my headache and body pain. Halo was in the bathroom just finishing up a shower when I knocked on the door.

"Good morning Joy. How did you sleep." I looked at him, "Ok I guess. I just have this headache that I'm trying to get rid of." "I heard about what happened last night. We will talk about it in a few. Meet me in the living room once you get yourself together. I want to talk to you for a minute."

After my shower, I walked in the living room to find that Halo had made me breakfast and placed some Advil next to a glass of orange juice for me to take. "Cola told me that you did good last night." I smiled, I guess I did. I left out the part about the Ecstasy pill just to avoid drama. Other than that incident these seem to be cool people, plus I needed a family and didn't want to create mess. As I began eating he started asking me more personal questions about school, family, and what plans did I have while being in this game.

"You can't be a hoe forever Joy. You got to want to do something better for yourself" "I know but it's just so much going on with me. You have no idea plus I'm not sure what it is that I want to do." "O yea. Tell me more ma." Shocked to know that he was interested in knowing more about me on a personal level. We talked for about a good two hours before everyone else started waking up. Amazing walked into the living room looking as if she had an attitude once again. "You didn't make me any breakfast?' Halo replied, "You were sleep and you know I don't like to wake you up. Don't come in here starting shit Amazing."

If looks could kill Halo would have been dead with the look that Amazing gave him. "But you can make this stupid bum ass bitch joy breakfast though! Wow!" I looked at Amazing confused. "She is sitting there with that dumb ass look on her face." One thing about me, I've never feared a female who picked with me constantly and I damn sure wasn't about to start.

"Watch your mouth please Amazing. You don't know me." "I don't got to fucking know you to know that you're a bum."

Halo finally told her to shut up and stop starting drama. Her best bet would have been to listen because I had so much anger pinned up it would have been bad for me to unleash my rage on her. "Whatever Ill make my own damn breakfast." I just sat there quiet trying to figure out why Amazing was so damn mean to me. If this is what having a wife in law was about I wanted no parts.

Cola came into the living room a few minutes later smiling and asking us if we were ready for tonight. "I already know Joy ready to make some money. We must take you shopping on Monday to get you some more clothes and shoes. Plus, we need to do something about that wig of yours lol. You can't be getting money with me looking crazy. Daddy you should have seen her last night! She did her thing!" Halo smiled, "I know you were telling me last night. Joy is going to be ok. I think she will like it here if Amazing stop fucking with her." Cola looked at Amazing scowling, "You gone fuck around and fuck with the wrong bitch one day and they are going to cut you. Stop your shit."

Amazing rolled her eyes and continued to scramble her eggs. Halo walked over to a stereo system that was in the corner of the room and turned some music on and started passing a blunt around the room. After we all ate and talked for a while, I opted to go and take a nap. I laid on the bed and took some deep breaths thinking about my next move and considering if this was something that I would settle for. It allowed me to see more of the city and learn how to really hustle just in case I ended up on my own once again. Plus, I had a decent place to lay my head and Halo and Cola seemed cool.

I've been dealing mouth smart mouth chicks my whole and I knew that if push come and shove, I would be able to smack Amazing if necessary, so she could leave me alone. I heard the door creaking open but was to tired to turn around to see who it was. I figured it was Amazing coming in to take a nap, so I just moved over to allow her to get in the bed.

I felt a warm arm wrapping around my waist and I turned over to see Halo kissing on my lower neck. "Whoa! What happens if someone catches us." He continued kissing me. "Don't worry about that. You belong to me now and I can do whatever I want with you. Cola is sleep and Amazing isn't here. You have nothing to worry about. No one is going to be mad. They know what's up. I need to taste this chocolate."

I just laid there and allowed Halo to proceed to licking my pussy. He stayed down there for about a good hour and once he was done I was in ecstasy. I felt so relaxed. I thought that he wanted to have sex but instead he wrapped his arms around me and kissed my forehead and we fell asleep.

Cola woke me up around 11:30 and told me that it was time to get dressed. "Amazing seen daddy in the bed with you so she got an attitude. She gets jealous sometimes like that's her man. So just ignore her. We are going to be in the Bronx tonight and shit don't start until 2 so take your time getting dressed and doing your makeup. I've already washed your outfits and packed your dance bag for you so don't worry about that."

I laughed and told her thank you. So now I finally found out what Amazing's issue was. She obviously wasn't a team player. But what I did know was that if she pressed me there was going to be some serious smoke. All I was trying to do was survive until I figured out what's next.

As usual, I took a shower and did my hair and makeup. I met Cola and amazing in the living room and we walked out the door, on our way to the Bronx to make daddy happy. Cola asked me if I wanted to take another E pill. "No, I think I'm straight. I'm not nervous anymore because I already know what to expect. Plus, I don't like the hangover. I just need a red bull though and ill be ok."

We stopped at a corner store that was across the street from where we were going and after Cola came out of the store we headed upstairs to get to work. We were inside of a two-bedroom apartment in a Co-op that didn't have any furniture. One room was used for a dressing room and the other VIP.

By the time we all got dressed and hit the floor it was crowded, and money was flowing. There were only about ten dancers there, so I knew that it was a great opportunity to rake up. I was clam and amped up off my red bull and ready to go. The night ended up going smooth as intended. Money was made, and everyone was happy at least I thought so.

For some reason once we were in the car Amazing decided that she wanted to start her bull shit. She turned around in a drunken spur, "Your stupid as fuck if you think daddy actually likes you. You out here all confident like you're the shit. Just because yall fucked don't mean shit." Cola jumped in and told her to once again shut up. I just sat in the backseat quietly smoking my Newport.

The whole ride home Cola and I just sat there listening to Amazing yell and scream on why she hates bitches. She got so emotional and started crying and telling me that she liked me, and she just don't want no one else around her man. We finally reached the driveway and I couldn't be happier.

Once we were inside I handed Cola my money bag and went straight into the room to get my things together for a shower. I overheard Cola and amazing arguing and decided to stay out of it. Halo came down the hallway asking what was going on. "This bitch Amazing drunk talking shit and I'm tired of her. She thinks she's supposed to be the only bitch around you. She keeps popping shit to Joy trying to run her off."

I just went into the bathroom and took a shower at that point. I did not want to get into that conversation. The argument got heated and I could hear them yelling over each other while I was in the bathroom. I heard Halo tell Amazing to pack her shit. After that it was yelling and screaming and suddenly, the bathroom door was kicked open and Amazing starts swinging on me while I was ass naked. I was caught off guard but eventually regained myself and beat the shit out of her.

By the time Halo broke everything up, I was crying from anger and Amazing had blood all over her face still yelling and popping shit. "I'm going to catch your ass on another day bitch. Don't let me se you anywhere." Halo yells, "Didn't I tell you to get the fuck out? Go get your shit so I can drop you off at the train station and I don't give a fuck where you go." Cola dragged me into the room and closed the door, "Are you ok? You don't have to worry about her mouth anymore she's out of here." "I'm good just pissed the fuck off. I didn't even do anything to that girl and she came at me crazy like that. Sorry for fighting in your house but I'm not a punk and I fight very well." "Lol, I see. Get some sleep though. I'm going with daddy to drop her off at the train station to make sure she doesn't try anything else. Don't worry about that shit that just happened though your good." After Cola left out of the room I just stared at the ceiling one again in disbelief at the luck I was having. I couldn't believe that I just got into a whole fight for no reason. Little did I know, it was only the beginning and it only got worse from there.

CONFESSION AND TIP NUMBER EIGHT:

MOST PEOPLE THAT YOU SEE FLOSSING LIVES OFF OF SECTION 8 AND FOOD STAMPS. DON'T BE EASILY IMPRESSED. #ISSAFRONT

It was exactly one week before my eighteenth birthday and I couldn't be more than happy with Halo and Cola. Every since Amazing had left, Cola and I have had a care free and drama free nights. Halo had taken me shopping a few times and I stayed with the latest shoes, clothes and hair trend. Halo and I had gotten so close that I even opened to him and told him about what I was running from and going through in NC. He didn't even seem shocked and had even gotten me a fake ID. Everything was all good at least I thought so anyway until one morning when me and Cola came in from work and, I was told I had to leave.

"What do you mean I have to leave? What did I do? I'm making money, I'm not starting any trouble, what happened?" "Its not you Joy. The kids are going back to school and we have been behind in our rent and now we must go back to the shelter to renew our section 8. Is there anywhere we can drop you off? If not, Halo will take you to a hotel and pay for it for a week and give you money for food and transportation. You know how to get to the undergrounds, so you can still dance and make your money."

I was so pissed off to the point where I couldn't even ask what they have been doing with all the money that we were making and not to mention the fact that I was once again all alone. I had no choice but to pack my bags and allow Halo to drop me off at a hotel.

While we were in the car, he told me to promise him that I would take care of myself and stick to my goals and get myself together. I told him I would as I held back tears and fear of being alone with no hope once again. He dropped me off at a run-down motel on Queens blvd, not to far from one of the underground strip clubs where I had been dancing on the weekend. As promised, He paid for a week and gave me $1000 for my pocket to hold me over until I figured out what It was that I wanted to do.

He suggested that I saved my money and trap out of the hotel until my birthday the following week and then find a nice room to rent. After he paid for the room, he gave me my room key and a hug and told me to keep in touch with him and Cola to let them know how I was doing. I walked in to my hotel room and hit the bed so hard I almost missed it. Here I was, alone, confused and lost. I was wishing that I could just call my family and just tell them everything that I had been through and to please just let me come back home but I knew that wasn't possible. I had made my bed, and sure enough I was going to lay in it.

I decided to take the night off and start from square one tomorrow. I was so emotional and knew I had to put together a solid plan to make it at least until the following week. That way I could get my ID and try to find a room or studio apartment. I promised myself that I would stay strong, work hard and stack my money. Every bone in my body was independent and I had made it this far already alone so, I could pull myself up out of this. On top of that I knew how to hustle. I learned from working the clubs that I had a knack for talking men out of their money without even breaking a sweat. Most of these tricks were thirsty. Being that I was young, with smooth chocolate skin and a nice smile, they would do pretty much anything just to sleep with me and I knew it.

I winded up taking a long hot shower before I laid down for the night. I turned on the TV and decided to watch the news and catch up on some current events. I haven't watched the news in what seemed like months. As usual, it was a bunch of lies and drama going on. I started thinking once again on my future and what It held for me. I just wanted to be happy, loved and to get myself together. I knew I was destined for something other that this life that I was beginning to grow tired of already. I had been in NY for only a short period of time and had been through so much. One thing is for sure, I had gotten tough and my southern accent had disappeared quick. I had no choice. It was either get tough or be bullied and ran over and I wasn't having that. I laughed to myself out loud as I thought about it all and finally drifted off to sleep.

The next morning, I woke up with a headache from crying to so hard the night before. Its like my body was on autopilot and I was starting to wake up with headaches. I automatically took a hot shower, got dressed and walked to a near by corner store. The only problem was, I had only been outside at night and all my clothes were work clothes so of course I was getting all type of cat calls during the short 3 block walk to the store.

I guess I had officially turned into a hoe and you could just tell by looking at me. Once I was inside the bodega, I picked up some snacks and waters to keep inside of my room. I had only been eating once a day, so I didn't have an appetite for food anymore. "Yo papi let me get a pack of Newport shorts and some Advil." "Mami how old are you? You look young." "Don't worry about that just ring my shit up so I can get out of here."

The neighborhood that I was in was a Spanish one. There was Spanish music coming from all over the place and the store was filled with sweaty men who were dressed in construction clothing. One of the guys followed me outside and begin to talk to me. I already knew what he wanted by the way he was looking at me. Before he even had the chance to speak, "What's up papi. You want to come with me to my hotel room? You got $100?" "Where your hotel at, I want to go with you I have lot of money." He showed me the inside of his wallet and I thought what the hell. Mind as well get back to work. I had a goal and I couldn't stay in this hotel forever.

It was only about 2'o clock and he was already drunk. I could smell the coronas on his breath and coming out of his pores. I didn't care. Even better for me. I knew he would come quick and then I could go about my day and figure out where I wanted to work at that night. Once we were in the hotel room, I took my Advil and told him to get undressed. "Wait a minute mami we party a little bit yes?" He took out a bag of cocaine, and wad of money out of his wallet and dumped it all over the small table next to my bed. It wasn't anything that I haven't seen before and told myself fuck it, at least I can charge him for the hour. He had the money, but I wanted him to give me my portion before he got to high to forget. "Yo papi do your thing I don't care. You want to spend an hour with me? Give me $160." "No mami I stay for a long time. I give you $500 until tonight. I just want a pretty girl while I party."

I couldn't believe that once again luck was on my side. I already knew that he wouldn't be able to fuck me or even want to while he was high. Easy money for me. I turned the small radio on and lit a cigarette as he sat there sniffing lines. "Mami you like to dance. Come dance with me we going to have fun don't worry." "No papi no dance just enjoy yourself." And for the next two hours he did just that. He was so high, all he could do was sit there and stare at the window. I would try to touch him, and he just laughed and said noooooooo. I could care less.

Time was moving, and it began to turn dark outside. I knew I had a long night and had wanted him out, so I could take a nap and get ready for my night. "Alright papi you gotta go." His drugs were gone, and he just sat there making this annoying sniffling noise and blowing his nose every two minutes. "Ok mami I leave now no problem. Can I come back? Ill give you whatever you want." "No papi I got to go to work thank you. Here's my number. Call me."

After he left, I cleaned up all the remains that he left behind. I had $1500 and being that it was Friday, I knew I could turn that I to $2000 effortlessly. I laid there filling like there was hope after all. I would use that week to stack as much money as possible before I did what I had to do to get a ID on my birthday and find a room for rent.

After I woke up from my nap, I did the usual routine. Shower, dress, hair and makeup. I called at taxi to take me to the spot where I would be dancing at that night. I found a spot in the bathroom under the sink to stash my money, grabbed my dance bag and headed out the door. Once I was inside the club, I got dressed and hit the floor.

I had a whole lot of determination inside of me which turned into a successful night. I had made over $600 and decided to head back to the room. At that point it felt kind of good to be on my own. I could work whenever and however I wanted to and spend my money however I wanted to. I didn't have anyone hoovering over me and I could count my money by myself.

"Im at this hotel right here baby. Thank you." I gave the taxi driver a $10 bill, grabbed my dance bag and headed upstairs to my room. For some reason I had a bad feeling in my stomach and of course Ignored it. As I was walking down the hall way to my hotel, I noticed that there was someone walking behind me, so I stopped. It was a tall, black dude wearing all black and some timbs. I already knew that he was trouble because it was hot outside and he had on Timberlands. I didn't want to walk to my hotel room just incase he was in fact following me. That way he wouldn't know my room number. I looked at him as I stood to the side and pretended like I was having a conversation on my cell phone. I looked out the corner of my eye as he started to walk past me. I noticed that he had his hand in pockets and before I knew it, there was a nine-millimeter pointed at my stomach.

I already knew what time it was as I stood there looking at him shaking my head. I was doing so good and now here we go with more bullshit. "Open the fucking door and don't say shit." "You don't got to be aggressive sweetie I already know what time it is. I don't have much money on me. You can have whatever's in my pockets." Surprisingly I wasn't even scared. It was something about him that gave off the impression that he wasn't going to shoot me. Probably wouldn't even put his hands on me. "I said open the fucking door." I had already known from previous incidents that if I screamed for help no one was coming. I obliged and opened my room door just hoping that he would take the money and just leave and not rape me.

"I've been watching your ass for the past three days. You out here hoeing with no pimpin what the fuck is wrong with you. Yea its pimping bitch." O no! Not this shit again. Here we go. I sat there quiet waiting for him to make his next move. I didn't care what happened. I just knew that he wasn't getting any of the money I had stashed away. He could have the $600 that I had made that night and that was all. I decided that I would just go with the flow, just so I wouldn't get robbed or beat up. I knew I had to trick him into thinking that I would choose him and then find away to get away from him.

He picked up his phone and called someone, "Yo, come upstairs I'm in room 311." O no. "Hoes like you gone learn to not be out here without no mother fucking pimpin. It's crazy Kev baby you gone choose up today." I sat there quiet letting him rant and rave about his cars his hoes etc. A few minutes later, two black females walked in to the room. I could tell from the dirty flip flops and stiff wigs that they weren't getting any real money. I didn't even care to ask for their names. At this point, they were a joke to me.

"You see these two hoes right here, they been loyal to me for three years now and they are happy. You are joining a winning team baby. Whats your name beautiful. "They call me Joy." All I could do was shake my head because I knew from the way this conversation was going that I was in for a long night. I didn't care. Just as long as my money was safe, and I ended up back at my hotel or another one without any scars or being robbed it was ok with me. I had goals to achieve. I had to survive.

CONFESSION AND TIP NUMBER NINE:

THE FIRST THING THAT YOU NEED TO LEARN HOW TO DO WHEN HOEING IS LIFE IS LIE, AND LIE GOOD

After about ten more minutes of pointless ranting Crazy Kev finally told me to pack my stuff because I was going home with them. I should have won an Oscar with the role that I was playing. "Ok let me just pack my stuff daddy." I walked into the bathroom and closed the door quickly stuffing my stash money inside of a condom and shoving it deep inside of me. I even took three hundred dollars from the $600 that I had made that night and added it to that.

After I was done, I started shoving my things inside of the large suitcase that Halo and Cola had given me to keep my things in. All four of us walked outside and Kev instructed me to place my suitcase in the back of his beat-up Toyota. I looked at his car and almost laughed thinking to myself, "you out here pimping, and this is what you're driving." I kept my comments to myself and continued to play along. "So where is my new home and how are we getting money?" "Bitch we are going on the track tonight. You need to make daddy some money before you walk into my house." Nina looked up, "What house?

Joy we live in a hotel just like you were." O hell no. "Bitch shut the fuck up, who was talking to you." Kev seemed to be be bothered by the fact that Nina just blew him up. I could tell that she was bottom because she was sitting in the front seat with the same attitude and presence as Cola had with Halo. But this time it was raging with disrespect and I could tell that Nina and Trina weren't happy at all. Hell, I wouldn't be to if I had to wear dirty ass flip flops.

"Ok, so were would I be keeping my suitcase at while we work?" "You can keep your shit right here in the car." I figured I would go on the blade and catch a few dates. That would at least allow me to go into their room and sneak out with my things once they were asleep. "Ok daddy." "O you a good hoe? I can tell that you aint green either with yo fine chocolate ass. You probably be out here making all the money." I just smiled. I was tired and ready to get the hell away from these washed up bums. "So what blade we going to Sutphin?" "O no baby girl we play on Broadway." I had only worked Broadway twice since I been in New York. I hated going there because it would always make me paranoid that I would run into Omni.

Broadway was right in front of the Ocean Hill projects where that dirty girl lived that I met when I first arrived. I had learned the area quickly and just told myself that I would stay on the back blocks and just work those instead. "Where your phone at Joy. Put my number in it and if you have any questions while you out here working call me. I'm known in these streets and aint nobody gone fuck with you." Yea Yea whatever dusty Ive heard it all before. I knew damn well that Kev wasn't getting as much respect as he says he was. Not with these washed hoes and busted car. Not to mention the fact that they were living in a hotel and probably had been for a while. I hadn't been hoeing long but I knew these types and I knew to stay far away from them. They probably were spending the money all on drugs and liquor. Fucking bums.

"Don't even think about running off. Remember I got your shit bitch. Now get out and go make me some fucking money. Nina and Trina going to show you how real hoes get money." I looked back at those dirty flip flops that they were wearing and laughed so hard in my head I almost got a damn headache. Hopefully it was another hotel near them, so I could just crash there for a day to clear the smoke from them once I snuck out. There wasn't a snow ball chance in hell that I would be staying with them. Not even to figure out a next move. I could do bad by myself.

Kev dropped us off at the corner of Broadway and Moffat. It was already 3 am and I was tired and ready to get away from itchy and scratchy. The three of us started our trap by walking straight up Broadway. I was thirsty to catch a date. I knew that Kev wasn't a real threat or even a real pimp. I still had all my stash money. He didn't even think to break me.

We had to have been the only girls working or it was busy because there were no one else in sight. About ten minutes past by and Nina and Trina had caught a double date. I continued to walk for about five more minutes before noticing a money green BMW circling the block. Another five minutes went by and it was still circling. I figured it was a date and with the luck that I had been having now that I was on my own and the fact that he was driving a BMW he should make for a real good date.

He pulled over and I quickly ran to the car and jumped in the passenger side. It smelled like money and was very warm inside. He looked so damn sexy. Tall, dark skin, built with waves spinning. He was wearing a pair of black jeans, a crisp tee and a pair of fresh timberlands. I smiled, "Hey daddy, what are you looking for tonight?" "You know what I want. Joy, right?"

I sat there looking stupid while my heart fell in my feet. It was either he was a pimp, or I was becoming a famous hoe. How did I end up in this situation AGAIN? I was mentally smacking myself because now I had to figure out how to run away from not one but two pimps on top of having to get my suitcase from the other one. I didn't know what I was going to do I just know I had to think fast.

"O no, please don't tell me you're a pimp?" "Come on now Joy, you know I'm a pimp just like I know you're a hoe. Hailing all the way from NC. I know all about you baby girl. You need to come home and stop playing with these local lames that's out here ruining your name. I thought you was dancing what happened? Who are you with now that got you out here back on the streets?"

Believe it or not he seemed cool and I was getting very good vibes from him despite the fact that he just told me my life story. I wonder if I played along with him, would he be willing to get my suitcase from Kev and take me to his stable. He was smooth, so I know he had other hoes. Plus, I would probably have better luck running from him than Kev and itchy and scratchy. I couldn't help but to get a little smart to answer his question, "If you know so much about me already than you know I still am dancing and you would also know I'm with Kev now." At this point why lie. "You with that bum as nigga. Lol. Nah I can't even see you go out like that. I'm about to call him right now and let him know you choose." He was dead ass serious. "Yo Kev what up this Cash. Joys with me now." He hung up. "So, what's up Joy you are coming home or what." "Ummmm, yes but he has my suitcase in his trunk." "Say no more." He called Kev back and told him to meet us at the corner the corner of Broadway and Moffat, so he could get my clothes.

While we waited, Cash looked at over at me smiling with a mischievous smile, "Joyful, Joyful. Its about time we have met. I'm Cash for the record baby girl. Now let me ask you something, if you come home with me, how long are you going to stay? I don't just let anyone come into my home. I like you.

From what I heard about you your ruthless just like me and my other hoe Fire. You see baby girl we don't play by the rules we make our own. I already know about you as I told you before. So, there's no need to explain anything. So, are you ready to be loyal to one? Are you ready to be a real hoe and take this shit all the way? Are you ready to come home and have your own room in a clean house? You ready to stop struggling and really get on your own?" I had A gut feeling about cash. But it was a good one. So, I choose. "Yes, I'm ready." "Say no more. I promise you your making the right choice and were going o be together for a long time no matter what. Let me run and get your shit from Kev."

After cash got back into the car, he made another phone call to my new wife n law Fire. "Yo get up lazy and get the other room clean. Remember the girl Joy that I was telling you about? She's coming home." After hanging up the phone Cash asked me once again was I ready. I laughed and told him yes and thanks for getting my clothes from Kev. "O no problem. He was a little salty, but he'll be alright." We drove for about fifteen minutes before we pulled up to a three-family brick home in East New York. The neighborhood seemed quiet and was kind of clean considering where we were. I had known ENY to be hood. But I guess this block wasn't.

Cash grabbed my suitcase out of the trunk and walked me up to the front door. As we were walking in there was a tall dark skin woman with dreads walking out. "Yo Tisha what's up?" I could tell that she was gay by the way that she was dressed.

"Aint shit, getting ready for this shift, who this?" "This is joy, joy say hello to your new neighbor." I smiled, "Hello." "I hope you don't walk heavy like this other one. Geesh. Fire walk around like she got ants under her feet all damn day." I laughed. "Nah you know she gotta be dramatic all the damn time. Come on Joy so you can get settled and sleep. I know your tired."

We walked up a flight of stairs to a metal door in the middle of the hallway. Cash opened the door to a clean two-bedroom apartment with a cute Pitbull named caramel barking at us. "Sit down caramel. You scared of dogs." "No, I love dogs! Hey baby." I sat, and petted Caramel as Cash walked my suitcase to the back of the hallway. There was a opposite bedroom right across from what I had known to be my bedroom. The door opened and out came this small petite short light skinned girl with a bright red lace front on. This must be Fire. "Heeeeyyyyy Joy welcome home." She had on a matching red bra and panty set with at least 15 tattoos in various places with a few piercings and grey contacts in her big bright eyes. Wow was the only thing that I could think. She was edgy and pretty and the opposite of me. I just knew that we would get along great.

"Hey ugly, you finally bring me a wife n law that looks at least half decent. Joy you should see the raggedy ass birds that he be bringing in here. Them bitches be hit, and I have to show them the door like nope." Me and cash laughed together. "Shut up Tweety. I'm going to get breakfast while yall get acquainted. Fire show her her bedroom. Joy get a list of any hygiene products that you may need."

Cash took our breakfast orders while me and Fire sat in the living room that had been decorated with two black couches and an entertainment center that was cattycornered and talked while she rolled and smoked a blunt while we talked. "So how old are you? How long have you been in NY? Do you have any kids?" I answered all her questions shyly and of course lying about my age before she proceeded to tell me that she had two kids that lived around the corner, she was 26 and she had been with cash for four years now.

"Damn that's a long time. You must really like him." "I love that little ugly nigga. I would do anything for him. We believe in nothing but loyalty in this house. He's a good dude. You will see. You get your money however you want to get your money and he will ride for you no matter what. We are a close family here. You will be fine. Have you met Biggs yet?" I shook my head no. "He lives upstairs. He's a bouncer at a club but he's also one of Cashes best friends. If you need anything and daddy not around, ask him. He will get you whatever you want." I just smiled and bobbed my head to the music that was playing through the speakers.

For some reason I had already felt comfortable around Fire and in the apartment. It was almost like I belonged there. "We usually go out of town once a month and while in NY I usually just play Sutphin or Back page. Daddy gets his own money, so he will never press you over a slow night." So far, they sounded like my type of people.

Fire got up and escorted me to the back and showed me my room. There was a huge queen-sized bed in the middle of the medium sized room and a full-length mirror near the door. There was a small tote that she told me to put my things in until they got me a dresser. Fire then told me to come and see her room. She opened the door and I had almost passed out. It was filled with shoes, bags and wigs neatly surrounding a queen-sized bed. Once again, I was wowed and knew from the looks of her and her room that I was in good hands.

"There are only two rules in this house. We don't go in each other's rooms and you must take a shower as soon as you get in the house. Got it?" "Yea I think I could manage that." "Good. Do you need a bar of soap and wash cloth? I had plenty of hygiene and wash cloths in my suitcase and told her no. I went into my bedroom and dug through my suitcase to find what I needed for my shower. I grabbed my things and took a nice long hot shower reflecting on the day.

I almost forgot that I had stashed money inside of my pussy. I pulled out the condom and just like clock work Fire came busting inside of the bathroom. All I could think of was fuck. I hope she didn't see me or know what I was doing. "Its just me Joy I gotta pee. Daddy's back with breakfast to. Hurry up before your food gets cold." She flushed the toilet and washed her hands before closing the door. That was a close call and I'm glad that I didn't get caught. Cash seemed like a nice guy but, I highly doubt he would be nice after finding out I was stashing already. I like them and was comfortable but, I had to make sure I was straight at the end of the day.

After my shower I met Cash and fire in the living room. We all sat at the table and had begun eating our food. "You gotta excuse ugly. He eats like he's still locked up." I looked up at Cash and he was surely eating fast like he was in the mess hall and he didn't wasn't anyone to take his food. "No, I'm just trying to hurry up and eat so I can get away from your stinking ass." I bust out laughing and was relieved to see that these two joked and played around a lot. "O before I forget Joy, here's your new phone. Me and Fires numbers are already stored inside of it. Text me some thigs that you like to eat and drink and whatever you need so I can pick it up while I'm out. And before you go to sleep we need to talk."

O shit do he know that I was stashing already? Had fire said something? I mean I know she saw me. The shower curtain was clear. I just smiled and shook my head yes as I finished up my French toast and scrambled eggs. We all sat for about thirty more minutes talking about everything from the current events in the paper to the newest song that hot 97 was playing. After while we all started yawning and Fire stood up and told us we were going to sleep. She grabbed a juice from out of the refrigerator and went into her room and closed the door.

"So how much money do you have for me Joy?" Shit he knew. "I'm not going to put my hands on you or anything, but you know the rules of the game. You know you must break. I know you done had a few pimps, so I tell you what. What ever you give me will be put in a safe. If you're not happy here in a month you get all your money back plus a ticket to where ever you want to go." How could I argue with that? Cash seemed like a man of his word, so I obliged and gave him the condom stuffed with money. "Lol, that's how yall doing it now? Damn."

He left the money in the condom and walked over to the entertainment center where he opened a safe and placed the money inside. "I know your tired so I'm not going to keep you up. I got some errands to run. Make yourself at home and don't forget to text me what you need." "Ok, yea I'm calling it a night. I guess ill see you when you get back." I went into the bathroom and pissed before I went into my new bedroom. I heard the front door creak open and close shut and had knew that Cash was now gone.

I walked into my new bedroom and jumped up on the bed to get comfortable and heard a loud boom as if something had hit the floor. My first thought was that I had broke the bed frame from jumping on the bed so hard so of course I looked underneath to see the damage that I had done. I pulled up the bed spread and saw something that seemed to have been wrapped up in a small blanket on the floor. I slid the object to the end of the bed and touched it, curious as to what it could be. I picked it up and couldn't believe it. I was holding a 45.

CONFESSION AND TIP NUMBER TEN:

IF IT LOOKS LIKE A GUN AND FEELS LIKE A GUN LEAVE IT ALONE. ITS NONE OF YOUR BUSINESS

A million questions started going through my head. Was this mine? What was it doing under my bed? They had to have known that I was going to find it. I mean it was under my bed after all. I pushed the gun back under the bed. It wasn't the first one that I have seen, and I knew it wouldn't be the last.

I knew I was being nosy, but something told me to look in the closet. I opened the door and saw that Cash had been using this closet for his clothes. I also noticed a yellow envelope in the back of the closet. I opened the envelope and started looking through court papers that belonged to Cash. It seemed like he was fighting a case for assault and was on parole for attempt murder. I sat there shocked but smiled because I knew I had a real one on my hands.

I put the papers back in their place and got back on the bed. All I kept thinking was did I finally make a good decision. I had been bouncing around from place to place since I been in NY. It couldn't be that bad here with Cash and Fire I mean she had been with him for four years after all and he seemed real and genuine. Plus, once again there was a roof over my head and I would be taking care of.

I promised myself yet again that I would make the most out of being with Cash and see how far that he was willing to go with me. I shot a quick text to Cash letting him know my favorite drinks and letting him know I didn't need anything else. Finally, it was time to go to sleep.

I woke up around 8 pm. I was so tired and the only reason why I had woken up was because I had needed to go to the bathroom. After I washed my hands I went into the kitchen to find Cash and Fire in the living room plying a video game. Fire had changed her wig and was wearing a bright blue lace front with curls and of course a matching bra and panty. Cash was showing his muscles in a tank top and a pair of jeans with socks on.

I smiled as Fire looked at me, "Look who decided to wake from the dead. Lol." "Joy you have plenty of food and snacks in the fridge help yourself. You were snoring by the way." Fire started laughing, "Damn sure was. You must haven't had any good sleep in a while." I was kind of hungry, so I smiled and went inside the bathroom to brush my teeth and wash my face. Should I tell them about what I found underneath my bed? They have kept it real with me so far, so I worked up the courage to tell them.

I looked inside of the refrigerator and low and behold, there was bottles of water and my favorite snacks. Wowed once again I grabbed a bottle of water and a snicker mini and sat on the couch. I didn't know another way to say so I just said it. "Your gun fell from underneath my bed. I didn't know what it was, and I put it back under there." "O I already got it. And I see you found out that I'm on parole. Its no big deal with your nosy ass. Just remember, curiosity killed the cat."

How did he know that I went through his paper work? Was there a camera in the damn room somewhere? Had to be. I nervously shifted on the couch. Fire looked back at me, "I hope your not scared. Daddy's a gansta and then a pimp. Just know that you will always be protected Joy." I just lowered my head and ate my snicker while playing with Caramel.

"So, where y'all want to work tonight?" Fire answered, "Sutphin for me." I figured I would just go along with it. "I already know your no stranger to Sutphin Joy, so you already know what time it is. Don't worry about no one fucking with you either." I had heard that one before. "Just get your money and if a pimp come at you tell them your daddy told you to tell them to suck you dick and stick your middle finger up while you're at it." He was dead ass serious. This should make for an interesting night.

"What are you wearing? Let me see." Fire paused the game and walked me back to my room. "I'm not sure. Probably a black dress and since we are going on the blade some flats incase we have to run." "No mama we don't wear flats to work. Gotta keep it pumped up bitch you not green you already know. Put this on with those black heels I seen you pull out last night." She picked up the tightest skimpiest dress I had in my small wardrobe. "Make sure your hair and make up is on pint to wifey. We are the flyest." She wasn't lying about that.

By the time we were all dressed and showered, Fire was pushing through in a black dress with cut outs, a pair of black and gold apple bottom knee boots with fishnets and a long black wig with bangs. She had done her eye makeup in Gold glitter and had even added gold jewelry. She looked bomb. "Yall ready to go make some money? We can stop and get something to eat on the way to the blade. Joy what you need to drink? You look a little nervous you ok?" "Yea I'm ok." But I wasn't. I had a bad feeling about this night.

We all got into the car and stopped at Wendy's and ate in the parking lot before we hit the blade. "Joy, you're with me now your good no matter what ok? Call me if you need me. You and Fire find a spot to meet up at together when yall get tired and ready to go. I'm always close by so don't hesitate to use your phone."

I said ok as me and Fire got out and started our night. "O shit there goes my regular. Right on time. Ill catch you later Joy be safe." I started my stroll and decided to stop at Sutphin and 113th to smoke a cigarette as I waited for a date. There was plenty of cars passing by and I couldn't figure out why no one was stopping to pick me up. Shit I know I looked good and I was ready to make some money.

I heard my boost mobile chirp go off. It was cash, "Yo get off the corner and meet me in the back blocks I'm picking you up its hot out here." I chirped back, "Ok but what block." I got no answer, so I just turned around and walked down 113th. I walked about two blocks before I saw Cash driving. For some reason he kept going and I turned around and seen why. The D's had pulled over and turned the lights on. Lord please don't let me be getting locked up. I just knew I was done for.

"Put your hands behind your back." Once again, my heart fell to my feet. "I said put your hands behind your back." Shit. I was being arrested. I knew that if they ran my name that they would see if I have warrants and send my ass straight back to NC. I placed my hands behind my back as I was placed inside the back seat with two other undercover officers. I knew better than to say a word and they didn't have much to say either.

We pulled up to the 113th prescient where I was placed in a holding cell. There were only two other guys there and myself. I didn't even bother to sit down on the dirty brown bench that looked and smelled like someone had pissed all over it. It was disgusting in there. Just like the other cells I had been in while I was locked up in NC.

The same officer who had arrested me came into the room and opened my cell. He walked me back up to the front desk and told me to wait while he gathered some papers. "O shit here yall go locking up the hoes lol." A near by officer jokingly said while talking on the phone. "Yall need to let them hoes make their money. They not hurting nobody." "Yea I know, It's the bum ass neighbors that keep calling and complaining. Just take your ass to sleep. Look, lets make this quick. I want to go home. What's your name, address and DOB?" I told him the first name that popped into my head, "Denise Williams, I just moved up here, so I don't remember my address and my birthday is 9/9/86." "You sure because if your lying to me we are going to have a long night and I don't like long nights."

I had heard that they lock you up in Juvenile detention until you turn 21 in NYC and I damn sure didn't feel like fighting no bad ass little girls. I knew they were going to extradite me back to NC, so I would be on the infamous Rikers Island for a while. That was the first birthdate that popped I my head so that's what came out of my mouth. I answered, "Yes that's it." "Alright let's get you finger printed so you can catch this next bus to central bookings. Its going to be cold and be prepared to freeze your ass off in that little ass dress your wearing."

After I was finger printed the officer allowed me to get Cash number out of my phone. Surprisingly, I wasn't questioned and had even been allowed to talk on the phone for a while. I wasn't dumb though. I knew they were listening. I called Cash, "Yo cuz I'm locked up can you come get me?" "I know some body already called me and told me. Don't worry, I'm coming to get you as soon as they give you a bail I'm there. You trust me?" I had no other choice at this point. "Yes." "Good just keep your mouth shut and don't start acting all scary. You got this ill see you soon."

He hung up the phone and I just sat there taking all this in. This cant be life. About an hour later, the officer came back in and handcuffed me and the other two guys together and escorted us outside into a big van. Thank god that this wasn't my first time being locked up or I would have been scared. Everyone was staring at me.

"Yo watch your head and your ass in them heels. We don't need no law suits. And by the way Darcell, North Carolina said Hi." Shit I was caught. O well I made this bed so in it I shall lie. I knew that I would eventually get caught. We drove about ten minutes to central bookings. It was way more people inside. I was finger printed once again and escorted to a small cell. "Name and DOB?" "I had already forgotten the fake birthday I had given them and just said the name. "Denise Williams." Luckily for me the officer didn't question it and locked me in the cell.

This one was even worse than the last. On top of that, there were two crack heads sitting in the cell scratching and moaning loudly withdrawing from whatever drugs they were on. It smelled horrible in there and I couldn't take it. There was an officer sitting next to the cell. "Yo can yall move me please it smells crazy in here." "Shut up, no yelling." I looked shocked and pissed off as the officer turned her back towards me. This cant be life.

Two whole hours passed by of nothing but me watching the crackheads moan and nod off on the bench. I was still wearing heels and my feet begun to hurt from standing up the whole time. Finally, "Williams step out." I sighed with relief to only find out that I was being escorted to a larger holding cell that was filled with a little bit of everyone. There was a group of young girls who had been arrested for shoplifting, a few middle-aged women who were all staring with a blank stare and of course more crackheads.

"Yo look at this bitch." One of the young girls said while pointing at me. "What happened to your clothes." "She doesn't have any clothes she a hoe bitch shut up and leave her alone." I ignored it as I found a spot on one of the benches. I noticed that there were phones, so I walked over and called Cash back. He must have known it was me, "O they must got you in central bookings now." "Yea I'm here and already there are bitches starting shit." I looked over at the group of girls and behold, they were still staring at me. "You better hold your own don't be a punk. That's not a good look Joy." "I got this covered don't worry about that." "As soon as you see the judge and they post your bail I'm coming to get you no worries."

Cash and I said our good byes and hung up the phone. I went and sat back in my little spot on the bench while accidently kicking one of the crackheads that was lying on the mat." Damn miss you can't watch where you're going with them ugly ass shoes on!" Everyone in the cell laughed at the crackhead and I just sat there and rolled my eyes.

One of the young girls looked up, "We already know what you're in here for how much you be out there charging?" I looked at her and again rolled my eyes, "Mind your business." "Bitch please you don't want no smoke over here." I rolled my eyes again. "Williams lets go." The officer was calling me just in time. "Yo she just got here how she get called already we been in here for like five hours." The officer looked at the girl who was talking and replied, "Stop stealing from rainbow and you won't have to worry about that now shut up and take a nap." I laughed as I followed the officer into yet another damn cell. OMG. How many cells were there.

I was starting to get pissed off. Once inside I seen that there where four other girls and one has just gotten called out. "Good luck mama." I was curious, so I started asking questions. "Is she going home?" "She's going to see the judge, so hopefully. They locked her up for a blunt. Dumb shit. I already know what you're in here for so don't even tell me. I can tell by that cheap as dress and those shoes mama you got to do better." I looked at the old timer who had just threw a whole damn shade tree. I didn't even respond. Just once again rolled my eyes and sat down.

I waited for another hour praying that the judge would just let me out. "Williams step into the next room and see your lawyer." I walked into the adjoining room where there was a greasy looking guy in a cheap suit waiting to talk to me. As soon as I sat down, "I will be representing you. You are being charged with soliciting for the purpose of prostitution. This is not a serious charge and ill ask the judge to let you go home but if not hey will probably set a $500 bail." I didn't even get a chance to ask any questions before he got up and walked away. I just thought to myself wtf just happened.

I went back into the cell and finally shortly after my name was called to see the judge. Another CO opened the cell and instructed me, "Put your hands behind your back and go stand beside your lawyer." Once the door was opened I went and stood beside my lawyer while the DA called the docket number and requested a $500 bail. My lawyer begun to speak up, "This is Ms. Williams first arrest and she should be released without bail." The judge finally answered. "Set bail at $500." Just like that, I was on my way to Rikers Island for the first of many times.

CONFESSION AND TIP NUMBER ELEVEN:

IF YOU WEAR WIGS WHILE HOEING, MAKE SURE YOU GET IT SEWED DOWN SO IF YOU GET LOCKED UP YOU CAN KEEP IT AND SELL IT FOR COMMISSARY OR UN-WEFT IT AND BOX BRAID YOUR HAIR

After about four hours of waiting in another dirty cell, my name was finally called to be transferred to Rikers. At this point I was honestly scared. I was the only one who had been remanded with bail. Everyone else was sent home but I couldn't worry about that. I had bigger problems. I was getting ready to come face to face with all the war stories and crazy things that you hear about one of the toughest and biggest jails in the world. All I know is that I had to keep my mouth shut and protect my self if needed.

We finally arrived. After crossing the long bridge and driving past different jails we were finally at Rose M. Singer. This was the jail that was specifically for women. I stood outside with an escorting officer for what seemed like forever. The door finally opened, and I stood in a small foyer and was asked to go through a metal detector by a snotty looking CO. "Walk through slowly." I obliged. "I said slowly walk through again! Damn. You fucking hoes get caught sucking dick and want to come in here and act stupid." I looked at her like she had grown four heads and couldn't believe that she had the nerve to talk to me like that.

"What's your name and DOB.?" "Williams, September 1986." "You don't look 23 to me. I know your lying about your age. Stand in front of the camera so we can take your picture for processing. Afterwards turn around and step inside the cell behind you." I turned around and looked inside of the cell that was filled with once again, detoxing crackheads. I just shook my head and did what I was told to do.

There were about six other cells with different boroughs written over them. I was in the one that was labeled intake. There were only a few women in each one and I tried my best not to make eye contact. It smelled like rotten fish inside and out. There was only standing room available in the cell that I was in so, I stood up and rested my arms through the metal bars and looked around. It was so loud. All I could here was, "Yo what's going on with my bail? Where's the bus? Yo CO this lady needs a doctor! Can I get my meal please? What's taking so long?" All the while, about four CO's where sitting in the officer's station laughing and playing on their cell phones. From the sound of things, I was going to be in for a long night.

About another four hours (yes four hours) had passed by and I was weak from standing up and my ears were ringing from the nonstop yelling and screaming. "Williams, step out and go to medical." I was finally being moved. I was escorted to medical by one of the officers. As soon as I stepped inside, I was told to sit down for vitals and don't talk while I'm there. I wasn't surprised and had gotten use to the rudeness already. The nurses and doctors were all foreign and I just knew they were getting ready to use me as a Guiney pig and I had no choice but to let them. I received two shots and a TB test along with a pregnancy test and other screenings.

Afterwards, I was sent back to another holding cell. This time there were regular women in there who all seemed to be appalled and shocked to see someone like me in there with them. "Yo ma how old are you? You look like you need to be in juvi. What are you in here for? Your too pretty to be locked up. They gone love you in here." I looked at the older Spanish lady who had asked me the question in broken English. She had to have been speaking for everybody because I held the whole cells attention and they wee waiting for my answer. I blushed at the compliment before lying, "Me and my friend got into a fight." I damn sure wasn't going to tell them that I was there for selling ass.

"Damn ma, they be locking people up for dumb shit. I got into a fight with my next-door neighbor...." "Shut the fuck up miss. Don't nobody want to keep hearing this bum ass story." "I'm not shutting shit up. Tell your mother to shut up........." A CO came to the cell, "All you bitches shut the fuck up before your paperwork get pushed back and your asses be sitting here for days." "You can't keep us in here for no more than 24 hours CO." "Try me bitch. Now shut up!" I stood there dumbfounded at the level of disrespect being passed around and relieved that the attention was taken off me.

We all sat quiet before our names was called and we were told to grab a blanket and follow the guard to our housing area. There were so many inmates in the hallway. Some of the new admissions had been known and where speaking to their friends that were still there from there last bid. I was shocked to see that everyone was wearing regular street clothes and not uniforms. I had never seen fly inmates before where Prada and Maury sneakers seemed like it was a must to have. We arrived at our housing unit and waited for the CO to tell us our cells and I was tapped on the shoulder, "Excuse me miss, you trying to sell your wig? I need it to box braid my hair. I can get you whatever commissary and phone calls you need." Wait a minute, did this lady just offer me commissary for my wig? It couldn't be that serious but hey, I wasn't sure if Cash was going to leave me there to rot or come through, so I shook my head ok. I wasn't baldheaded underneath my long wig, so I had nothing to worry about.

It was around 4am when I finally was able to lay my head on the thin mat and metal bed. I was used to being locked in a cell, so it didn't phase me. What I was worried about was Cash and how I would get through this small bid if needed. I had no family and no support, but I did know how to hustle and use people to my advantage, so I would be good either way. I just didn't think I was ready to mix and mingle with the people from the NYC streets. I couldn't believe that I had once again found myself by myself. I had to do better than this. I couldn't even sleep with all the thoughts running through my head. Besides that, it was so loud with people knocking on their cell doors and yelling across the unit to each other under their doors and through the vents. All I heard was, "That bitch not ready to fuck with me. I don't want her anyway, her pussy smelt like fish yesterday bro." "Yo I'm trying to get that wig off that new girl." "My nigga did you see how sexy CO Charles looked today bitch that's daddy!" All these conversations were happening at once and it was making me frustrated. I haven't slept, shower or eaten anything in the last 24 hours and I needed a cigarette badly.

The lights came on and I heard the CO yell "On the door for breakfast" and loud clacking of cells being popped open. I thought this would be a great opportunity to use the phone to call Cash and see if he was going to post my bail, so I could get out of this hell hole.

He picked up on the first ring, "Yo" "Hey it's me, are you still coming to get me?" "Why you scared? Lol. Your bail was posted like an hour ago. This is NYC though so its going to take like 12 hours. Just play some cards and watch some TV until they call your name. You miss daddy?" This was music to my ears. He had come through on his word. "Yes, I miss you!" "I know you do. Yo hold your head Joy. I'll see you soon."

After we said our goodbyes I let out a large sigh of relief. "Somebody going home." I looked to my left and seen a slim, young black girl with a familiar face. "Don't I know you from the block? You Fires new wifey you fuck with Cash and them, right? I got locked up right before you did." "Yup that's me. I see they got you to. Your daddy coming to get you?" "No. This like my sixth time being locked up bitch. There's no more bell for me. They gone make me do 60 days. But look we about to get locked back in. Imma chop it up with you in a few hours. Are you coming back out?" "Yea I guess. I need to past this time by until I bail out. What's your name again?" "They call me Mocha."

We said our goodbyes as we walked back into our cells. I sat there for hours once again thanking God that Cash had came through on his promise and anxiously waiting to get off this rotten ass island. A few more hours passed by and the lights came on again. There was a different CO on shift this time around. You could tell he was lazy and had a long night. There had to be at least 20 inmates out around him and he was in the corner sleep.

I spotted Mocha coming out her cell. "Yo Mocha I'm trying to take a shower." "O girl get your bucket that they gave you and meet me in the showers. I'm about to take mine too." I went back into my cell and grabbed the bob barker soap and towel that was given to me in intake. I didn't have a wash cloth, but I already knew from previous jail experiences that the soap had lie in it and killed germs. All I had to do was wash my underwear and socks out with it and use that. Or just rip part of my towel. After my shower, Mocha and I talked about the day to day hoe shit that we go through. Being raped and robbed daily and having to put up with bitches and their attitudes. She seemed cool, but I had already known that she couldn't be trusted.

"Yo you play spades? I'm about to find two more people to play with us." "Ok cool." I went back inside my cell and got myself together. Mocha had given me some antibacterial ointment to put on my knees hands and lips and I was doing just that when my cell door opened. "Yo ma you trying to let me get that wig or what?" "On some real shit, if I get bailed out tonight you can have it ma. But please don't just barge inside of here like that." "My bad ma damn." This lady had some damn nerve and it couldn't be that serious over a damn wig.

After I got myself together I met Mocha and two older women at a small table. These women had to be in their late 50's, and I'm confident that this wasn't their first rodeo. They were way to confident and laid back. "Yall OG's ready to take this ass whopping?" "Yea whatever ma sit down, shut up and learn something." I laughed. I had been playing spades for years, so I wasn't intimidated by the older ladies one bit. We played a full game and of course the OG'S won. Until this day I know for a fact that they were cheating. Me and Mocha sat and talked all day long. She had been hoeing for a while and was schooling me on some ins and outs. Come to find out, she didn't even have a pimp. She had a baby daddy who was no good, and she was just out there trying to make ends meet. I felt bad for Mocha. But it was people like us who played the game and got it the worst.

After we ate lunch I heard the CO yell my name, "Williams pack your shit and get the fuck out." I couldn't believe it. I was finally free again. I ran inside of my cell and rolled all that shit up inside of a ball and ran to the front gate. Mocha and the thirsty lady who wanted my wig met me at the gate. I snatched my wig off and gave it to Mocha and told her to do what she wanted with it and followed the CO to intake to wait for freedom. After once again anxiously waiting and pacing back and forth for about two hours, I had finally boarded the bus and crossed the bridge. We stopped at a few more jails and picked up some men who were also being released. "Yo my nigga I can't wait to get a fucking cigarette and some pussy. It's been too long." Others where rocking back and forth and the rest of us were just staring out the window mentally telling this stink ass fucked up ass island to kiss our ass, while making empty promises that we would never return no matter what.

CONFESSION AND TIP NUMBER TWELVE:

IF YOUR WIFE-N-LAW DON'T CLAP WHEN YOU WIN SHES HATING.

On top of feeling like I had finally found a real dude to hold down, I was feeling free as a bird. Cash and Fire was waiting for me as soon as I crossed the bridge. "OMG you really came and got me! That was the longest two days of my life!" "Your welcome Joy. Just know that I need my money back. We are happy to see you too right Fire?" "Yea I guess." U oh. Here we go with the attitude from the bottom. I already knew what Fires problem was, so it was no need to even entertain her jealousy. Plus, Cash checked her off the rip.

"Yo, lose your fucking attitude." "I just don't understand how you can take money that I made and bail somebody like her out of jail. I feel some type of way." "First of all, miss know it all somebody like her broke more money on her first night than you have ever made in a week." Fire looked at Cash like she just swallowed a large pill. I didn't have the time or energy to entertain her now. I was way to busy basking in my new-found freedom.

"Yo Joy don't worry about her. We about to hut the road and go to Boston for a week. We will go shopping when we get there. It's a four-hour trip so rest up. What yall want to eat?" That made me even happier. I didn't have court for another two weeks so that seemed fine to me. Plus, I had never been to Boston and was excited to see what was going on there.

I took Cash advice and slept the entire time on the trip. I kept waking up here and there to hear Cash yelling at fire for trying to do mischievous shit to wake me up. She was doing every little petty thing to pushing her seat all the way back to, flicking her ashes from her cigarette in the back seat. Cash was checking her, but it wasn't enough. I made a mental note to myself to check her myself once we were out of his presence.

We arrived at a hotel right outside of Boston. Cash paid for the room and told us to go upstairs for a while and he would come back and get us, so we could shop and get ready to hit Blue Hill Ave. He gave us room keys and we walked upstairs. As soon as the door closed, I let my presence be heard. "Look fire, I've dealt with jealous bitches like you before and you don't scare or intimidate me ma. Stop with the bull shit." "Hold up Joy don't come for me. I didn't do anything to you." "O so you want to cry wolf when we alone? I'm not gone disrespect Cash and pop in front of hm. He already got a lot going on. Just stop being petty." "Bitch you just got here. You don't know what the fuck is going on." I got a little closer because clearly, she didn't hear me the first time when I told her to stop disrespecting me and watch her mouth. "Once again stop disrespecting me." She stood there looking at me for a brief second and then grabbed her cell phone and ran into the hallway. I could hear her yelling on the phone through the thin hotel walls. "Yo Cash come get your fucking bitch she up here threatening me for no damn reason. I didn't do shit to her." I wasn't fazed one bit. I had dealt with plenty of hoes like her before and knew that she was going to act crazy and then play the victim. Luckily for me, by the time I got around to Cash, and Fire I had mastered how to handle situations like these.

It was simple. After I noticed that Fire wasn't going to do shit but run her mouth and tell, I decided to take another nap. I was on foreign ground and I had to be well prepared for what was ahead.

An hour passed by and Cash and Fire came strolling inside the room. They were obviously talking about the brief confrontation that Fire and I had and what ever he said to her had left her pissed off and ranting. "Yo Joy what happened?" I looked at him with a side eye from the bed and played dumb, "What happened with what?" "Fire said you threatened her." "No, I didn't I just asked her could she please stop disrespecting me like we are not on the same team." "Look, both of yall cut it out." Fire was pissed. "Get yourselves dressed so we can hit the mall and get some clothes to wear while we are out here. Yall got a party tonight but that's later. Yall gone hit the blade after so make sure yall save all this crazy energy for later. We got work to do." I looked at Fire and smiled. I knew it would piss her off even more but hey, if this was the game that she wanted to play then so be it.

We all took quick showers and headed downstairs and got into the car. Fire sat in the front seat with her arms crossed and lips poked out showing just how upset she was. Me and Cash ignored her and enjoyed the scenery that Boston had to offer. Moments later we pulled up to the mall. It seemed small and I honestly have seen bigger but hey, once you live in NY, you don't get impressed easily.

We shopped for about two hours before heading back to the room. Fire was still pissed off and once again Cash checked her. "Yo what the fuck is your problem? You are walking around with this stank as attitude like someone did something to you." "You know what my problem is Cash! Every time we get a new bitch you always show favoritism with her and forget about me. You always take their side with shit like I haven't been with you through everything." "See there you go trying to run bitches off with that jealous shit. I'm a fucking pimp I'm not your boyfriend. I'm not going to tell you again to watch your mouth." "You aint gone do shit just like she aint gone do shit." I looked over at her and once again laughed. "Yea whatever Fire. What we doing now? If not nothing I'm taking a nap." "Joy please excuse her and yes take a nap. Its gone be a long night."

We woke up around 11pm and ran the usual routine. Shower, dress, hair and make-up. I had chosen to wear a gold long sleeved dress that complimented my now 5'7, 38DD, chocolate frame and paired it with some cream and gold thigh high boots and a long wig with a bang that brought out the shape of my huge innocent looking eyes. Even though Fire and I were beefing, I had to say that she slayed in head to toe red and black and daddy was looking just as sexy as we were. "Yall ready to make some money? I plan on going go carting tomorrow so make sure yall make it a good night, so we can go see what Boston has to offer" Shit. Sounded good to me.

We pulled up to a small building where the party was supposed to be held at. Me and Fire didn't have our dance bags but had bought passible lingerie from the mall earlier that day that we would just wear with our boots. Once we got closer we saw that this was a hood spot and it honestly looked dead. There were only about two cars outside and the building itself looked ran down. I looked at Cash, "Umm are you sure you got the right address this shit looks crazy." "Nah it does, I'm about to go inside really quick, don't let nobody car jack yall." Fire let out a small giggle and I was hoping that it was a sign that she had lost her attitude from earlier. I couldn't quite tell because for the brief two minutes that cash was inside, she played on her phone.

"That shit is a dub. I'm not letting yall work that shit. The blade is right around the corner though." Fire asked, "How do you know you don't even live here?" "Come on now bitch you know I done spun around the area and asked a couple of questions here and there earlier today. So, we are going to spend the block and I only want yall on these three blocks. Don't go no further. Same shit as NY. No hotel dates just stay right here. Police don't really jump out here so yall good." We both answered ok as he gave us our condoms. "Three dates a piece and we out. Yall be safe." Fire and I got out the car and Cash pulled off.

It was a gloomy chilly night with heavy fog. It honestly looked like a seen out of a horror film. It didn't scare me though. I pulled my thigh boots up and stayed on the curb while Fire worked the other side of the street. A tan explorer pulled up with a black driver, a white passenger and an Asian guy in the back. They seemed to be young but willing to spend money. plus, Cash was nearby, and we were staying right where they pulled up at so what harm could come. "Hey babies, any of yall pimps or cops?" The driver answered looking at me like I was a life-sized candy bar, "Hell no but how much for you to suck our dicks?" "$100 a piece but two of yall have to stand outside while I work and then switch." "O nah get in we got that." All three dates exploded in seconds as they took turns and got serviced. The date was over within twenty minutes and I had already made my short quota and could go in early.

But then the tables turned. After I finished servicing the Asian guy I the back seat, the black and white guy got in the front. Before I could wipe the spit off my face and even have a chance to get out, the driver sped off down the block while the Asian guy opened the back door and tried to snatch my wristlet and kick me out of the car. As I'm yelling and screaming, "get the fuck off me! Just let me out what the fuck", I noticed Cash following behind us.

The driver made another sharp right which sent my right leg flying out of the opened car door dragging on the ground while my left hand held on to the door and my right hand holding on to my wristlet for dear life. I had just busted my ass for this money and I wasn't letting go. The white passenger noticed that I was hanging on and jumped in the back seat and started kicking me in the face while and I had to let go. I hit the ground and rolled hard onto the side walk from the impact.

I was dizzy as I glanced up and saw Cash running towards me and yelling my name and kneeled and held me. "Joy wake up Joy. Yo Joy! Come on man its not that bad answer me" I started to come back around, and the pain started kicking in as I answered him, "Yo Im not dead but them fucking bastards aint get my money." I felt an excruciating pain from my right knee, my left shoulder and it felt as if though my jaw had been broken. I was afraid to even ask how bad my scars looked. I didn't even want to glance at them myself. I saw blood on the ground and knew that it was bad.

"Yo I'm about to pick you up and put you in the car hold on. I am so sorry Yo I thought you was good yo." "Its cool just get me out of here. How bad is my leg because it feels like its falling off." "Nah you just need to be thankful to be alive yo they almost ran over you. We gotta get you to the hospital just don't fall asleep."

Cash placed me in the backseat and pain shot up my body as I yelled. Cash jumped in the front seat and drove around the block and picked up Fire. "Yo what the fuck happened? OMG what happened?" I was surprised to see that she even showed compassion with what was going on. "She had a bad date nigga was dragging her out the car we gotta get her to the hospital. Fire I need you to talk to her to make sure she doesn't fall asleep. The hospital is about five minutes from here Joy hold on."

Fire yelled at me and ended up singing songs with me to help keep my mind off the pain and keep me from falling asleep. We arrived at the hospital and Cash ran inside and came back out with two nurses and a stretcher. They all helped me out of the car as the nurse asked me questions that I couldn't even answer due to the pain and Cash and Fire just shrugged at because they didn't know anything about me except for my first name. I quickly yelled, "My date of birth is 9/12/1990 and I don't have any allergies, insurance and I'm homeless and my name is Darcell Marshall." I had to give them the correct name and DOB just in case I died because it damn sure felt like I would.

I glanced down at my leg and saw blood dripping down my leg covering it from my knee to my foot. It looked as if though all the skin had been scraped off my knee cap and I also had blood running down my shirt from my shoulder. They got me onto the stretcher and wheeled me into the hospital fast as if I was on one of those TV shows while taking off my shoes and cutting my clothes off. A doctor showed up as the nurse repeated what she seen and the information that I had just given her. I started to feel dizzy again as the lights on the ceiling past me by. I could hear Cash and Fire screaming things at the doctor as they ran down they all ran down the hallway. I felt a small pain in my arm and looked and seen a nurse inserting a IV into my vein. In just seconds, I found myself drifting off into one of the most peaceful sleeps I had ever had.

CONFESSION AND TIP NUMBER THIRTEEN:

IF YOU WORK THE STREETS, LEARN HOW TO HIDE BEHIND THE CARS GOOD ENOUGH SO THAT THE POLICE DON'T SEE YOU.

I woke up the next day hoping that everything that has just happened was a nightmare but was quickly brought back to reality with the smell of institutional cleaner and the beeping sound of the IV and heart monitor that I was hooked up to. I looked down at my leg and surprisingly it was still there and only had a brace on it. I reached up to touch my shoulder and only felt a bandage. I had survived with minimal scaring. I said a quick prayer and thanked god that I was still alive.

A few short moments later I was met by a nurse. "Hello Ms. Marshall. There are some detectives from the local police department that are here to speak to you." O no. Not the police. The first thing I thought about was where was Cash and Fire and hoping that they didn't leave me here stranded.

Two white men in black and white cheap suits walked into my room. "Hello, we are just here to ask you a couple of questions about what happened last night. You got some harsh scars. Do you have any idea who did this to you?" I was hoping that if I told them that I didn't want to talk to them they would leave me alone. I mean after all I didn't live here, and I wasn't exactly in the right.

"No, I don't, and I honestly do not want to talk to you. I just want to go home please." It worked! The detective looked at me with a smirk while handing me his card that I dropped on the floor as soon as they left. "Well if you change your mind please call us. We are here to help." Lies. Lies and more Lies.

After the detectives walked out I grabbed my cell phone which I noticed was sitting next to me on the charger and called cash. "Yo come get me please I'm ok." "I know you good. I just left a few hours ago. Meet me downstairs after you get your discharge papers. I'm on my way." Cash has always been short on words and more on action and I was thankful for that. Lord knows I didn't feel like explaining and answering questions.

I got myself dressed and pressed the nurse call button so that she could take my IV out and discharge me. "O no miss you can't leave yet. The doctor would like to keep you here at least for another night for observation to make sure you don't have any bleeding inside…." I quickly cut her off. "No maam I don't want to stay. Please discharge me and take this IV out." "So, are you refusing medical treatment?" At this point I had an attitude. "Clearly."

About two hours later I was limping myself down the hallway. I had been instructed to wear the knee brace for at least two weeks and change my bandages twice a day. As promised, Cash was waiting for me outside with an angry looking Fire in the front seat. I quickly dismissed her attitude as I gave him a hug followed by him helping me inside the car.

"Yo first of all, please tell me what made you get in a car with a black, white and Asian dude. They don't even belong together. LOL. You should have known that was suspect." "I don't know man, I was just paper chasing. I didn't even think twice about it but at least we got a story to tell. Lol. Hey Fire. Its nice to see you." She looked at me and scolded me with a fake smile and turned back around with her lips poked out. "She got an attitude Joy don't mind her." I was used to it and once again dismissed it. "We about to drive back home though. I know you hungry. What do you want to eat?" "I don't even care at this point. Just take me anywhere. I got the munchies from them pain meds that they gave me. Did yall pack my stuff up that was in the room." "Yea we got everything don't worry about that. Just rest up and try to figure out a way you can make some money while you heal."

Did he really expect me to be outside or in a damn strip club working? I hope not. We stopped at McDonalds and ordered food through the drive through and hit the highway. I was still doped up, so I had no problems falling and staying asleep. I woke up to a slamming car door and noticed that we were back in Brooklyn. I mentally prepared myself to climb the flight of stairs and to think the pain away. Once I finally reached upstairs I went straight to my bedroom and plopped on the fresh black sheets and comfy pillow top mattress. Cash followed behind me with my bags.

"Yo Fire get dressed I'm taking you to Sutphin." I heard her yell back from her bedroom, "Whatever Cash. Check on your dumb ass clumsy ass bitch. Ill let you know when I'm ready." Now why was I getting violated once again. This girl just does not learn. Cash checked her for the millionth time, "Yo watch your mouth and hurry up. Joy never mind her. You know she's just jealous, but you also know that she's just mouth." "I'm not worried about Fire. I just want to go to sleep." "Look I know you need to rest for a day or two so I'm going to give you that. But mean time, you need to figure out how to make some money or get ready to hit the blade again. We took a heavy L in Boston and I need my money back." Cash hugged me and gave me a kiss on the forehead. "I'll be back in a few hours. Let me go put this bitch down. If you need anything before I get back text me and let me know." Cash and Fire left, and I went to sleep.

Four days later…

Cash and Fire had been arguing nonstop every since we got back from Boston. She and I haven't spoken one word to each other since. But on the flip note, it seemed like Cash and I have gotten just a little bit closer. We ended up having a heart to heart conversation that lasted a few hours and I'm glad we did. We got a better understanding of each other and I had even opened to him about my past.

I had gotten cabin fever and was ready to get back to work or even go outside for that matter. The past few days had consisted of me taking a shower, eating and going back to sleep. I figured I would start back working on Back Page for a few weeks before going back to the club or on the blade. I told Cash my plans and he was with it. He took some sexy pics of me in the living room and I must admit, my chocolate complexion topped with all hot pink lingerie looked good against the white walls and hardwood floors of the apartment. I smiled, "Cash let me find out you're a photographer to lol." "Nah, I wouldn't say all that I just know what men look for."

"Yo Fire get in here and let me get some pics of you. We are going to be working Back Page until Joy gets better. That way you can take a break from Sutphin." Of course, Fire had an attitude and stormed into the living room and held her head to the side. "First of all, I'm not working no fucking back page. You know I hate that shit. The only reason why you trying to make me is because this bitch can't fucking walk. I'm not doing shit Cash."

She stuck her middle finger up and turned and stormed back into her room after slamming the door. Cash sat there with a blank look on his face. I could tell he had finally reached somewhat of a breaking point but at the same time I was hoping that he wasn't one of those pimps who beat on their hoes. I had been through that enough. "Yo Joy go in your room please and close the door." All I head was loud noise and banging and Cash telling Fire to pack her shit.

Fire apparently didn't want to leave and before you know it she was back in her room laying on her bed was if nothing just happened. I walked out of my room to find clothes and bags scattered everywhere from our hallway and downstairs to the front door. Cash looked at me as I looked up and down the hallway from the living room, "Joy just get dressed please so we can go and make some money."

I obliged and a few short moments later me and Cash were sitting in the car on our way to Queens to post. Curiosity got the best of me and I had to ask, "Does this always happen with yall because I feel like it does." "Don't worry about it Joy." I clutched my invisible pearls. I couldn't believe that I was now getting attitude as if I had been in the wrong. I left it alone and sat there quietly as I waited for my phone to ring.

For the next two weeks Cash and I had been working non-stop on Back Page. Fire was starting to come back around with her attitude and started talking to me and Cash. She had opted to catch a taxi to the blade and worked alone while Cash took me out. My leg started to get stronger and I eventually lost the knee brace. I still had a limp while I walked but I was good to go and still in disbelief about what happened to me.

Fast Forward…

Cash had taken us shopping to prepare us for tax season. I had grabbed a few more pair of thigh boots and a few long jackets and short dresses and a few wigs. Fire was into the whole colors thing and it showed from her pickings. She always like to dress in head to toe of the same color. She was definitely and 80's baby from Brooklyn. I would be working back on the blade from now on which was a huge mistake. From the month of February all the way to the month of November I had been raped and robbed so many times that I became numb to it. Not to mention the fact that I had been arrested over 6 times for prostitution and had been known by every officer in the 113th prescient by name. Not to mention the intake officers at Rikers. I didn't care about them because Cash had always bailed me out. No matter how much the bail was. Cash had gotten to the point where he started yelling at me telling me that I need to learn how to hide behind the cars when I see the police.

On top of all those things I had been dealing with the raft of Fire. The closer that Cash and I had gotten, the worse she treated me. It was to the point where we had been doing petty things to each other. She even went as far as bleaching my clothes in the laundry, spitting in my drinks and food that was left over in the refrigerator and putting soda in my contact lenses. In return I snuck in her room and through away her favorite clothes, stuck her dildos in bleach and even lied on her a few times so that Cash could yell at her.

I had turned 19 and was yearning to get my license. Cash promised me that if I continued making money I would have my license within a month. He even helped me get a copy of my social security card and birth certificate so that I could have the necessary points to get my learners permit. He and I were tight, and he had even kept his promise. By the time the month of November rolled around I had my learners permit and couldn't be happier. Even though me him and Fire had our ups and downs, I don't think that I could have been happier without them and all our drama.

I had finally felt what it was like to be cared for unconditionally. So, I thought so any way at the time. Until one cold crisp autumn day, it changed once again for the worst.

CONFESSION AND TIP NUMBER FOURTEEN:

IF YOUR A HOE AND LIFE GIVES YOU LEMONS, DON'T SQUEEZE THEM JUST YET BECAUSE YOU NEVER KNOW WHEN YOU WILL NEED THEM FOR A RAINY DAY.

It was a cold Thursday morning and I had just finished working a long night on the blade by myself. Cash and Fire had gotten into yet another argument where her clothes were thrown to the door and she slept the night away peacefully. It had been a slow night, so I was tired from standing and walking around for hours. On top of freezing in a short dress and thigh high boots and a small leather jacket.

Cash had an attitude all night and I didn't even bother speaking to him. I had come straight upstairs, jumped into the shower and laid down on my bed. As soon as I started drifting off to sleep, Fire decided that she wanted to go into the living room and blast the music as loud as possible. I already had known she was trying to get to me and that day I let her. I was tired. I was tired of her, having to work the streets and tired of the predicament that I was in. I was tired of the police and being arrested raped and robbed almost every week and tired of the dirty stinky nasty tricks that I had to deal with every day. I had snapped.

I walked into the living room and Fire was sitting at the table eating a bowl of cereal. "Yo can you please turn the music down I'm trying to sleep. Did you forget I worked last night and you didn't?" "Joy take your ass to sleep. I'm not turning shit down. You will be ok. Please carry on." I don't know what came over me, but I flipped.

"Yo Fire I'm tired of your shit come out side and square up. I'm not about to fight you in this man apartment. Bring your ass outside." She looked at me and jumped up. We both ran downstairs. She was in front of me and I noticed that she had a pocket knife in her back pocket. Before she had the chance to turn around, I grabbed it out of her pocket, held her down by the back of the neck and stabbed her twice in her stomach. It appears time paused as I stood there in shock starring at Fire with blood dripping all over her yellow shirt and jeans.

Realizing what I had just done, I ran straight upstairs into my room and grabbed some clothes and threw them inside of a duffle bag. I knew I had to get away before the ambulance and police came. There was no doubt in my mind that Fire would tell the police.

Once I got to the front door I noticed that Cash had ran downstairs as well. He was upstairs in our next-door neighbor's apartment and had heard us and seen when I stabbed Fire. I looked at him in silence, "Yo Joy take this money and the keys to the car and get the fuck out of here now. Go somewhere far. Go down south." I was still in shock as he handed me a stack of money out of his pocket and the keys to our spare car. A silver 2001 Mercury. I looked at fire about to apologize as she held her stomach bending over, and she cut me off, "Joy go hurry up. The police and ambulance are on their way Go Now!" Cash looked back at me, "Get outta here now!" I shook my head ok while looking back as I walked to the car, threw my duffle bag inside, jumped in the driver's seat and sped off while listening to the nearby sirens that sure enough was on their way to the mess that I had just caused.

I ended up driving all the way to Richmond VA before I got tired and stopped at a local hotel right off the highway. I was panicking the whole drive down, shaking and crying periodically wondering if I had just killed someone. I had tried calling Cash cell phone and I was getting his voicemail the whole time. I honestly did not know what to do. I was scared and lost once again.

I pulled into the Hotel and checked in at the front desk. This was the hood with crackheads outside walking up and down the street looking for either a date or their next fix. I didn't give a damn. I needed to try my best and relax my mind and figure out my next move. As far as I was concerned, I now had warrants in NY and NC, no real license and was driving a car with fake tags on it after possibly just killing someone all at the age of 19. My head started spinning as I remembered all these things at one time. Only thing that could possibly help me at this point was Jesus.

The clerk at the front desk looked at me and must have noticed that I was in despair and asked was I ok. Of course, I lied and explained to him that I was just tired. "Ok well I gave you the best room in the hotel, check out is tomorrow at 11." I said thank you and walked out of the office and across the hall to my room. As soon as I opened the door, I was met with stale molded green carpet with a king side bed that looks as if the blanket hadn't been washed in months. Not to mention the cigarette holes inside the blanket. I was disgusted but had honestly seen worse. I knew that they never changed the blanket in hotels like this and knew to just take the blanket off. Thank god the sheets where clean. I dropped my duffle bag on the floor and noticed that I grabbed my hygiene products out of my bedroom and took a long hot shower.

Afterwards I sat on the bed and carefully planned my next move. I had grabbed my dance shoes and some dance outfits and decided that I would be starting all over again. I knew how to hustle. I knew how to post on back page and I knew how to dance. I wasn't afraid to be anywhere by myself, so I decided to make it happen by any means necessary. I plugged in the laptop and searched google for strip clubs nearby and came across club Remy. I looked at the hours of operation and noticed that they had day shift available. I put together a small plan. I would wake up I the morning check out of the hotel, get dressed, grab something to eat and go work. And if I didn't like the club, I would simply make as much money as possible and drive somewhere else and do it all over again.

I knew I had to continue to make money to prevent from going broke, so I set a small $300 quota which should cover hotel expenses, food and tip in. The rest I would stack. I also decided to stop at Walmart and get a prepaid debit card to keep my money on. I had been robbed enough and knew better than to keep cash on me. I promised myself to stick to the plan and even tried to shine some type of light on the situation telling myself that I had a car and could travel anywhere that I had wanted to go. Even if it was for work. I had been hoeing long enough to know that the same rules applied everywhere and if I stayed low key, I should be fine. I knew to mind my business and keep quiet. Don't be friendly and always watch to see if I was being followed. Being that I was alone I dismissed the blade unless I had gone broke and needed the money and that wasn't happening. I knew that I did in or outcalls on back page that I needed to make sure the dates weren't the police. I had known how to spot a pimp form a mile away and knew how to doge them if necessary. I had known to never stay in the same place while out of town for more than a couple of days. I had known to be tough and dismiss being scared.

I quickly dismissed the anxiety of what had just happened in NY and all the what ifs with the plan that I had just came up with for myself. I wasn't ready to go back to jail and I was going to run if possible. This time I would have something to show for it. On top of everything that had happened I was also tired of starting all over again alone. Things where going so good with Cash. Why did Fire have to push me to that point? Why couldn't she just be cool and dismiss her jealousy? I was just trying to be protected, loved and have a decent place to call home. Even if it was with a pimp. I called Cash again and got his voicemail. This time I just sent him a text message. I said a quick prayer, thought about my plan some more and promised myself to do better and to never end up in this predicament again and that I would use this opportunity wisely. I scrolled through google once again researching black strip clubs from NJ to Miami and everywhere in between and eventually, drifted off to sleep.

CONFESSION AND TIP NUMBER FIFTEEN:

ALWAYS KEEP YOUR GUARD UP AND NEVER TRUST TO SOON NO MATTER HOW NICE PEOPLE SEEM TO BE

I had successfully stuck to the plan and had officially made it in Richmond. I had stayed there for a week with no issues what so ever. I had stuck to the plan and decided that it was time to move on. I auditioned for club Remy and got hired on the spot for day shift and worked back page during the night. I stacked money and stayed out of harms way. I had still not heard a word from Cash and started to think that he didn't want any more parts with me. But that couldn't be true. He had given me his car. I knew that I would eventually hear from him again and I had plenty of money stacked up to make up for the mishap with me and Fire.

I kept my plan in motion and choose SC as my next destination. I had read good reviews about a strip club called The club and decided to make the 6-hour drive there. This time I would get an extended stay room and pay weekly to save some money. The rooms were equipped with a refrigerator and microwave that I would be able to use instead of eating out all the time.

I took the entire day on Saturday to go and get a fresh wig and to get my nails done. I had bought a few more dance outfits from a girl who sold them at Remy and being that I was only outside at night decided to pass up on shopping and just wash the clothes that I had at a local laundry mat and wear them. I was good to go.

SC

I arrived in SC Sunday afternoon. I had found the extended stay hotel and had even driving past the strip club where I would be working at. Thankfully it was only about five minutes from the hotel that I was staying at. I checked into the Hotel and said a quick prayer once I opened the door and saw that the room was clean and decent. It was smaller than what I thought it would be, but I was satisfied. There was a small full-sized bed with the usual hotel linen and a small closet beside it. Across from the bed there was a small table, two chairs and the kitchenette had a small refrigerator and microwave on top of it. The bathroom had a walk-in shower, sink and toilet.

After getting somewhat settled in I drove down the street to a Walmart and stacked up on hygiene products, makeup and got some groceries to hold me over for the week. The club didn't open until 8pm so that gave me time to repack my dance bag, eat and take a nap.

From what I learned from the strip club in Richmond shit was a little different in the south. I had to hustle a little bit harder being that almost every girl that worked with me had the whole fake ass and titties thing going on. I had been in good shape and had toned up from the long walks that I use to take on the blade plus I was young, on top of the fact that I was focused so I was able to make it happen.

After my nap, I woke up around 6pm to get myself dressed and to make sure I had enough time to make sure my makeup and hair was flawless. I decided to wear a black long-sleeved dress and some cute sandals. I had gotten a long lace front wig in Richmond and flat ironed and styled it so that it looked more like a weave. Once this was done I jumped in my car and headed to The Club.

I pulled up to the club and noticed that it had just opened. There were only about four cars in the parking lot. It was a good thing for me. the club didn't close until two, so it gave me time to scope it out and get familiar with the rules and what you can and cannot do. I parked my car near the door, grabbed my dance bag and made sure I had my ID and everything else I needed to work. As soon as I walked into the double glass doors I saw the baddest strippers I had seen in my life. They all were standing around a white guy who I assumed was the owner in the office laughing and smiling with him. I took this as a good first impression. At least they were friendly.

I walked up to the small hole that separated the lobby form the office and smiled, "Hi I'm here to audition." The girls looked at me and laughed. My smile faded, and I tried to figure out what they were laughing at. The owner looked at me over his wired rim glasses. "You got your ID?" I shook my head yes, "Give it to me so I can make a copy. Meanwhile get your ass in the back and get dressed and make some money. We don't audition here. We hire anybody that wants to work so it gives our customers a variety. What your doing still standing there?" The girls laughed again as I stood there shocked at the straight to the point response from the owner.

A light skin small petite girl who had been wearing a pink blinging two-piece g string outfit with a matching wig smiled at me, "Come on, Ill show you around. My name is Fire. What's your name with your pretty chocolate self. Matter of fact we will call you Onyx." I looked at her and smiled. How ironic was it that her name was Fire? But I thought about the name choice that she had given me and it fit. After all Onyx was basically a black gym and if I was anything I was that.

Fire opened the main door to the club. The club was huge inside with seating for at least 100 people. There was a huge stage in the middle of the floor with a long 18-foot pole in the middle. I looked towards the back of the club and saw a smaller stage with mirrors in the back of it in the corner and a red curtain which was used for VIP and three small rooms for that were used for champagne rooms. The club had official lights and smoke machine. The only mishap that I had with the club was that it had concrete floors.

Fire looked at me and smiled as I took in the décor of the club. She escorted me to the huge dressing room before giving me the club breakdown. "So basically, you do whatever you want. You get on stage if you want to, you can smoke, VIP dances are $30 a song and champagne rooms are $125. Once again you do whatever you want. The money days are the weekends and we usually have over 30 girls from all over the place working. During the week its slow but you will still make money because its only about ten girls here and its tax season. We close on Monday and Tuesday and on the weekends the club closes around 6am so make sure you bring your red bull or whatever you do. We don't sell drinks here because we are able to go nude. Ill introduce you to some more dancers later. We are all close here. You look young. How old are you Onyx?"

I took all the information in and realized that she had just asked me a question. "I'm 19. Ill be 20 In September." "O wow your young as fuck. Most of us are at least 25 but your gone be our baby. We gone make sure you straight." I couldn't believe how friendly and open Fire was. I couldn't help but wonder if there was a motive behind her being nice. I would keep my guard up just in case. As bad as I had needed to vent to someone who could relate, I knew people from the south were nosy and I didn't need my business all over this club.

"So, this is the dressing room of course. Meet me back in the office once you are dressed." I smiled and told her ok. For some reason I felt nervous, but I quickly shook the feeling and got dressed. I decided to wear a black and white one piece that I had bought from Richmond with slits throughout it. It showed of my huge boobs and ass and hid my small belly. I did a double take in the mirror and made sure I was on point and opened the door and walked into the office to find smiling faces staring back at me.

The owner handed me my ID and smiled even harder once he looked at me in my dance clothes and stilettos. "You're going to do well here with them big ass titties you got girl. LOL" Fire looked as she was laughing "Damn sure is. Damn I didn't even see all that up under that coat." She introduced me to the other two girls that were in the office. There was a light skinned toned girl with a huge butt and a long weave wearing all black named Shine. Then I was introduced to another light skin plus sized girl who was wearing half pink and half black two piece. She was wearing her natural hair in curls and was very pretty. She looked at me and smiled and introduced herself as Harmony.

They all were so pretty, and I could tell that they were pros. We all sat there and talked until the customers and a few more girls started coming inside. It was show time. I walked back inside the dressing room to touch up my hair and makeup before hitting the floor. The music was loud, the customers were generous, and the girls were friendly. By the end of the night I had made an easy $500 and a few friends.

As the club closed, Fire invited me to eat breakfast with her, Harmony and Shine. I agreed. After we were all dressed and still laughing about our night we hopped in our cars and met each other at a waffle house that was right across the street from my Hotel room.

As we sat down I noticed that Fire looked at me with curiosity. "So where are you from and where are you staying Onyx?" I looked up and smiled only giving her straight forward answers while looking at the menu. "I'm from NY and I'm staying right here at the extended stay hotel. Before you ask yes, I'm alone. LOL" "O no I wasn't trying to be in your business or anything, I'm just trying to get to know you a little better that's all." Harmony chimed in, "Bitch we are being nosey and making sure your ass isn't down here to be doing no crazy shit. LOL."

After a few more questions were asked, we ate and talked and got to know each other even better. Fire had a daughter that she was taking care of all alone and was originally from Florida. Shine was from Queens and had been living with her boyfriend and Harmony had a new born son and was originally from Texas. I still had to stick to the plan and only told them what I wanted them to know about me. Just so they can feel as comfortable with me as I felt with them. After we ate, we all said our goodbyes and went our separate ways. It was three AM and my feet were killing me. Once I parked my car and went upstairs inside of my room, I quickly got undressed, stashed my money, and showered. I was so tired that once I laid down, I fell asleep almost instantly.

CONFESSION AND TIP NUMBER SIXTEEN:

WHILE WORKING IN THE STRIP CLUBS, STAY AWAY FROM OLD HOES WITH DRINKING AND DRUG PROBLEMS.

After working Sunday night and feeling the club out I decided to use Monday and Tuesday to lose the wig and go and get my hair done and rest up. I googled a black salon and went to the hair store, purchased some long human hair and got a sew in. While I was getting my hair done I felt my phone vibrating in my pocket and looked at the caller ID and seen that Cash was calling me. I excused myself with excitement and took my conversation outside.

"Hello! Omg Cash what's going on? I'm in SC......" I was cut off, "Look Joy, Fire almost died. She just came out of a coma after three weeks Yo you almost killed her. She didn't tell the police what happened so your good. She's going to be down for a while though. Thought I would let you know. Where you at? What you been up to?" I was relieved to hear that I was in the clear with that situation, but I still had prostitution warrants to worry about on top of bail jumping. "I'm in SC. When I left NY, I stopped in Richmond for a week and worked a strip club out there and then came here. I found a club her and worked yesterday but its closed-on Monday and Tuesdays. I miss you so much Yo I was worried that you wouldn't call me or didn't want anything to do with me anymore."

"No, that's not the case. You think I would have given you the keys to my car if I didn't plan on calling you again? I told you from day one Joy I'm loyal. I will never leave you stranded. What have you been doing with your money? You got some money for me?" I know this would come. "Yes, I got some money for you lol. I knew that you would ask. I've been stacking my money and pretty much what I didn't use for hotels and expenses I've just put on a prepaid debit card. You know me. Better safe than sorry." "That's what I like to hear. I knew you would do the right think weather I was there or not. That's why I fuck with you Joy. But look, do you like the club and city that you are in? I got people down there in SC and I'm thinking about coming down there once Fire gets out the hospital." "I think I like the club but if not, you know I can always post. You want me to stay here? I got an extended stay hotel room and it's like an efficiency. Its pretty comfortable." "That's what's up Joy nah stay there. I should be able to come in about two weeks. Just continue to stack your money and stay out of trouble until I get there. How's the car been treating you everything good?" "Yes, everything is good with the car. I had no problems what so ever with it." "Alight that's what's up. I know you were worried and all that. Remember your good man. I used to do business in SC, so you should be good there. I gotta get off this phone and handle some business. Ill call you some time tomorrow. Your still my bitch?" "Yes, daddy and ok. Ill talk to you later." We said our good byes and I walked back into the salon to get my hair finished. Now that I had known that Cash was coming to be with me, I had to do what I had to do and go a little bit harder and stack a little bit further.

Once Wednesday rolled around I was ready to go. Cash had called me twice since the last time we have talked, and my confidence was at an all-time high. I went into the club glowing with my head held high. I had gotten there early to be able to pay the $10 tip in and get myself going. I had found out on Sunday that you could do dates in the champagne room. That avoided having to leave in and out of the club for dates. I was set and ready to go.

I said my hellos to the owner and went inside the dressing room to find Fire, Harmony, and Shine already there along with another dancer name Mya who seemed to be cool with them as well. They had already been drinking and I saw fire pop a pill out of the corner of my eye. I spoke to everyone and proceeded to do my make up and style my hair. I was minding my business and focused and hoped that the girls didn't think I was dubbing them. I had my mind on nothing but money and wasn't even ready for the small talk.

The girls carried on with their conversation and occasionally, when the conversation was brought to a whisper I knew that they were talking about me. I didn't even care. I knew how to be fake to blend in with them if needed and theses bitches weren't ready for my type of smoke. This is exactly why I kept the answers to a minimum on Sunday.

Fire had to be the one to say something, "Onyx sitting over there acting all funny and quiet. What's wrong your nervous again?" I looked at her through the mirror, "O no. I'm just staying focused and keeping my mind on my money."

As soon as I spoke my piece, I grabbed my money bag and headed on the floor. I didn't need anyone breaking my focus. I had noticed an older white guy sitting alone and approached him. "Hey baby how is you. I'm Onyx. How about we start off with a dance as we get to know each other a little better." He looked at me and got straight to the point. "No dance for me how much is VIP?" "You need everything its $125" He reached in his pocket and pulled out exact change. I told him to hold on as I walked to the office and gave the owner $25 for the VIP room. Me and my date followed him to the back and he unlocked the door and let us inside.

I sat him down on the small couch that was inside the room after he had pulled his pants down. I took a condom out of my money bag, put it on his small erect penis and began to suck his dick. That was the fastest $100 that I have ever made in my life. After about two good sucks he came. I kissed him on the cheek and told him thank you, grabbed my money bag and went back to the dressing room to freshen up.

When I got back inside the dressing room Harmony was in there alone. "Just to give you a heads up, that was Fires regular that you just did a VIP with and she is pissed off." As soon as she told me that Fire came bursting inside of the dressing room. "Bitch you done lost your mind taking my money. You already overstepping your boundaries." "Wait a minute Fire, don't raise your voice at me please and how the hell was I supposed to know that he was your regular did you forget I just started." She looked at me in an angry drunken spur, "Yea whatever. You are cut the fuck off already don't say shit to me. I don't give a fuck. Stay out my way. You aint gone make no money fucking with me." I rolled my eyes and proceeded with what I had been doing as she walked out and slammed the door behind her. Being that she came at me the way she did, I decided to cut everybody throat. Don't threaten my money. I had shit to do.

For the next two weeks I busted my ass in the club. I didn't have any other beef or words with any of the girls. Even when the weekend girls came, I just came to work, got dressed and made my money and went back to my room. Fire was bluffing because once the regulars familiarized my face, the money started coming in more and more.

I was still in contact with Cash and Fire had finally gotten out of the hospital. I got hooked on speaking to him every day. Being able to use him as an outlet really helped me get over the daily bull shit that happened at the club. I had needed a break from the club and couldn't wait for him to come down and join me, so we could go somewhere else.

Monday morning came around and I was awakened by a loud knock on the door. It was Cash. I didn't even allow him to walk into the room before bombarding him with a hug. He was dressed in a white tank top, jeans and his usual fitted hat with a pair of timbs. "Damn Joy let me come inside. I'm happy to see you too. Go brush your teeth before you say anything else. LOL." I had finally let him inside and he put his bag down and sat in the chair that was placed the small table in the kitchenette. "OMG I can't believe that you are here! About damn time I miss you!" "I miss you to Joy."

Being that we had talked on the phone every day we were pretty much caught up with everything. He looked at me with a serious look on his face. "Sit down Joy. We need to talk." I sat at the top of the bed so that I could use the head board for support for my back and faced him. "You already know that Fire is going be down for about two months healing. She's at her mom's crib right now. We ended up giving up the apartment. So much bad shit done happened there we had to go. After you stabbed her the police started coming and sitting at the corner watching the building. We got another apartment off Pitkin Ave so don't worry about that. But what I need you to worry about is are you really down for me?" "Of course, I am. I'm not leaving you Cash." "Good. That's what I wanted to hear. Listen, I got some work that I need you to help move in these clubs. It's only going to be E Pills and a little white here and there. I'm going to teach you how to work the scale and everything. You already said that they get it popping in the club you at, right?"

I looked at Cash with a blank stare on my face. Did this man just asked me to sell drugs for him? OMG. After going through everything that we have been through this far I thought what the hell I mine as well. After all, it would help, and I wouldn't have to catch as many dates and I had been trying to catch in the club. "Don't worry I'm going to stay down here with you for a while and I'm going to be putting in work as well. You trust me, right?" "I'm down and you already know that I trust you. I don't even know why you asked that question." "You already know that's what I wanted to hear. Come here and sit on my lap."

Cash and I have never had sex before, but I had a feeling that that was about to change, and I was right. I sat on his lap and he picked me right up and laid me on the unmade bed. I had slept in a bra and panty so there wasn't much to take off. I was nervous but that quickly changed once he turned me over on my stomach and entered me without notice. I had never made love before but had gotten a taste of what it was like that morning. After we were finished I laid there with a glow as he got in the shower. Once he was done I took a shower and got back in the bed and laid my head right on his chest and we both fell asleep.

Cash woke me up around 11am. I looked up to find that he had a scale, coke, pills and some saran wrap on the small table. "Wake up sleepy head it's time to work. Go wash your ass and check your breath and come see me when you are done." I gave him a smirk that matched his smart comment.

After my shower I had sat at the small table all ears and eyes and ready to learn. Cash wasted no time and I had learned everything that I needed to know in a matter of minutes. "As far as the pills are concerned you sell them for $10 a pill but no less than $8. Now with this white I need you to be extra careful. I'm going to send you to work with 125 grams. Its 28 grams in an ounce. A little more a little less depending on the customer. An ounce is $20. You should be able to get five ounces out of 125 grams. When you get a sell, go inside the bathroom, take out your scale and put some wrap on the scale and push the power button. When you see the scale is at zero, carefully weigh out an ounce, put the rest of your work up and wrap the ounce up and tie the wrap. That's it. You think you can handle this?" "Yes, I got it. It's not nothing that I haven't seen before." "I know that. So, go ahead and show me exactly what you are going to do." I mentally went over step by step and showed Cash that I could handle this. My only concern was stepping on whoever was already selling in the club.

After I showed Cash that I knew what I was doing I expressed my concern with him and he reassured me that I was good. He would be I the club on some nights with me and that I had nothing to worry about and to just remember what he had taught me and to keep my mind on my money. "Come give me a hug and look me in my eyes and tell me you got this." I obliged and found myself wrapped in his strong muscular arms, looking into his eyes. "I got this"

CONFESSION AND TIP NUMBER SEVENTEEN:

STUPID IS WHAT STUPID DOES, AND REMEMBER LOVE IS NEVER AN OPTION WHEN YOU'RE A HOE

Cash and I were a success in SC. Once I got the hang and balance of dancing with a little hustle on the side I was unstoppable. Cash ended up having to be either in the parking lot or in the club to make sure I had enough extras to move.

We had been in SC for a little over three months and the weather had started to change. I had gained enough regulars through dancing and extras to not even have to go as hard as before. I just went inside the club, ignored the bitches, got dressed and stayed focused. Cash and I relationship had taken off on a whole nother level. I had caught deep feelings for him and had even told him I loved him a few times. He had become more than a pimp to me and I now knew what it felt like to be one of those girls who fell in love with a guy and will do any and everything for him. Even though deep down inside I knew that the feelings weren't mutual. I didn't care. The love and attention that I had been receiving from him blinded me from the facts. Until, "You ready to take a break from SC? I need to go back to NY for a while and settle some things. You can come back with me or you can stay here. You're a big girl, you don't need me." "Actually, I do need you and I think it's time for me to take a break. When are we leaving?"

I had never trapped so hard in my life and to be honest with you it was easy. The club had already provided the clients and I didn't have to do anything but open my mouth and they were sold.

Unfortunately, Cash had to head back to NY for a while. He had needed to check in with his parole officer and Fire had healed and was ready to get back to work. "Do you think that It's a good idea for me to be coming back around her after what happened? We are doing good here why can't we just stay here Cash?" "Come on now Joy, you know you can't stay in one place to long. On top of that Fire got some new bitches for me in NY. We are going to come back down here in about a month or so. Have I misled you so far?"

It wasn't that I thought that cash was misleading me. It's just that I had been doing so much better alone and didn't care to go back to NY with the drama and bullshit that other bitches had to offer. Especially new ones that had been around Fire and got adapt to her attitude and bad ways. I wasn't worried about her retaliating towards me from me stabbing her. If pushed come to shove I would do that shit again and again until she learned to leave me the fuck alone. Cash and I had been doing so good together and had gotten closer than we had ever been. But, I knew that he was a pimp and I had respected the game enough to know that I had to share him. No matter how much I loved him. We packed, and I said my temporary goodbyes at the club. The next morning, we were headed back home.

After looking around at the random crackheads and fast walking people I was kind of happy being back in NY. I knew that I still had the warrants from missing court, so I had to move extra careful until we left back out of town. On top of that, my 20th birthday was right around the corner and I be damned if I would be spending another birthday locked up.

We pulled up to a brick brownstone right off Pitkin Ave. Cash pulled over beside me, "Yo I got to go see my PO really quick. The door is open and Fire and them are inside. Yo already got cash on you so if you need to step out for anything you good." I looked at him and rolled my eyes. Lord knows I wasn't ready to deal with the drama that was ahead of me. I grabbed my bags from inside the trunk and kept my mind on taking a hot shower and going to sleep. I knew that I still had to work later that night on top of keeping my eyes open for drama, so I would be needing my rest.

I walked up to the basement apartment door and walked inside and was welcomed with loud music and weed smoke. Here we go with this again. Fire ran to the door, "O I thought that you were daddy. What's up Joy?" "Hey Fire, what's going on?" I looked down at her stomach and saw the scar from the damage that I had done and cringed. She must have been reading my mind and my facial expressions. "Don't worry it don't hurt. Lol. We got two new wife n laws though. They are in my bedroom. This is only a one bedroom, so I guess you must sleep on the couch. Daddy said that he was getting you a hotel room, but I guess you can sleep here until he does."

This was all news to me. Cash never mentioned the fact that I had to sleep on the couch or even in a hotel. I could have stayed in SC for this shit. "Yea I guess. I'm about to take a shower and get some sleep though until he gets back. Can yall just try to keep the noise to a minimum?" I had never seen Fire move so quick before in my life to turn down some music and I was thanking god that this wouldn't be an episode from last time.

She came back out of the room with our new wife n laws. Cinnamon was tall and brown skin with small titties and no ass what so ever and had the nerve to be wearing one of Fires old stale brown wigs. She was followed by Sky, a light skin girl that was decently shaped and was wearing her real hair in a ponytail. Both looked basic and couldn't have been making any money because Cash would never allow them to walk around with us looking like that at any time of the day.

They both looked at me and smiled and Cinnamon who I had a feeling was the leader out of the two spoke up, "OMG! Hi wifey we heard so much about you! We can't wait for you to teach us how to work in the strip clubs!" I looked at her and mentally shook my head and just said the first thing that came to my mind, "O I see you ready to get some money! Its nice to meet yall too! Where have yall been working at Fire?" "We just been on the blades. Daddy said he didn't want us in the clubs until you got back so we just been outside."

Here I was once again being blindsided. Cash had promised me that I would not have to work with anyone else and I could stay to myself. I couldn't wait to see him later. I sat and played nice and talked to everyone for about an hour before I couldn't take it anymore. I had a feeling that Cinnamon and Sky was going to be trouble and that they weren't going to stay with us long anyway. Fire told me that she had met them in the Bronx and they both were thirsty to come home with her. Plus, they were both around Fires age and I knew form experience that they were running from a pimp somewhere. Cash and Fire probably peeped it too and that had to be the reason why Cash hadn't spent any money fixing them up. But those weren't my problems. I just wanted to get some sleep and I excused myself, took a shower, got comfortable on the couch and did just that.

I was woken up a few hours later by laughter coming out of Fires room. I saw Cash's wallet and keys laying on the kitchen table and knew that he had came home and was in the room with them. I had needed to talk to him and honestly didn't care what he was doing. I went inside my suitcase and grabbed my toothbrush and brushed my teeth and washed my face and quietly knocked on the door. "Come in Joy what are you knocking for." All three girls laughed at Cash dry humor.

I rolled my eyes and opened the door and almost threw up form the smell of a threesome and green weed and the sight of cash laying in the middle of it all. I was honestly kind of hurt and had known how Fire had felt. But unlike her I had respect for the game and quickly dismissed the feeling of jealousy. "Yo cash I need to talk to you please." He looked at me smiling, "Give me a few ill be in there." While I was waiting for him to come I decided to go ahead and start getting ready for my night.

Cash walked into the living room naked and I couldn't help but look at him and laugh. "Go take a shower them bitches stink lol." "I know right but on a serious note what's up." "Cash I don't want to work with them. I need to do my own thing and you forgot to mention this small as apartment and the fact that I had to stay in a hotel. If you are taking me to a hotel, can you just give me the money and I go now? I don't want to be here." His smile turned to a frown and I could tell whatever I had just said made him mad. Before I knew it, he had been in my face with his hand wrapped around my throat. "Yo Joy what the fuck is your problem. This is how your going to act now. Your going to start this jealous shit? This what we doing now? Setting bad examples for bitches now?"

I couldn't for the life of me figure out what had just happened so fast. Cash had never put his hands on me before and I just sat there in shock trying to figure all of this out. I was speechless and just stood there looking in his eyes filled with anger as mine filled up with confusion and tears. What did I do or say? What was going on? What happened that fast? I thought we had gotten close and had an understanding! He finally took his hands from around my neck, "Yo get dressed. You are taking them out tonight. Take them to Sutphin and Broadway and make sure everybody gets at least four dates a piece. Them bitches are to break you at the end of the night you understand?"

I just stood there and shook my head yes still in shock from what just happened. I can't believe Cash had put his hands on me because I asked him a question. I snapped out of my shock and grabbed my toiletries and went inside the bathroom to shower. I sat on the toilet thinking and replaying what just happened to try to get an understanding of what was going on. Did Fire lie on me again and make him upset? What would make him suddenly put his hands on me? The bathroom door opened, and Cash walked in and stood in front of me as I looked at the floor and listened to what he had to say.

"Yo Joy you have responsibilities now. I need you to help me with these bitches while I hold down my part. You already know I got other shit going on, so I need you to hold down this in. they are going to listen and do whatever you tell them to. We already spoke, and everybody understands that If you speak than its coming from me so you're not going to have any problems out of anyone." He grabbed the bottom of my chin and pulled my face up. "You still love me? Your still my rider." After all of that I was stupid in love and confirmed it by shaking my head yes.

CONFESSION AND TIP NUMBER EIGHTEEN:

BEING IN LOVE AND RIDING FOR THE WRONG PERSON WILL LEAVE YOU BROKE, HOMELESS AND LOCKED UP

As expected, Cinnamon and Sky only lasted for about three weeks and of course I was the blame for them leaving. Once they left, Fire kept blurting out that they would have stayed if Cash would have been more involved with them instead of having me drive them around to get money and catch dates. I can't front, I enjoyed not having to work but the two months that we had been back in NY had worn me out and I was ready to go back down south and was happy once Cash announced that we would be going back down south. This time we would be in Greenville SC.

My 20th birthday had come and gone and even thought I didn't do anything special, I was happy to be alive. I was 20 years old and already a seasoned Hoe and couldn't believe how far I had come with this game. I had known how to hustle and get it in with the best of them. I had come a long way. "Joy I need you to put Fire on to how the clubs work down south." I looked at Fire, "You never been down south before, right?" "No but I hear that's it's a lot of money there." Fire and I had gotten close since I been back. We hadn't had any beef and was often on the same page when it came down to Cash and working. It was a relief. "Pretty much all your doing is dancing, and you can do your dates in the club instead of having to go get a hotel room. Same shit, different state girl. On top of that you don't have to worry about any Pimps chasing you down. Just don't get to friendly with them bitches in the club. They just nosey and want to get in your business to gossip."

I explained to Fire all the ins and outs but still was worried about her. She was slim and really didn't know how to dance and being that this was the south that we were in and not the north, she had everything going against her.

Cash and I had been in a few arguments here and there and our relationship was beginning to get shaky. It seemed as if he was always stressed out about stuff. I couldn't for the life of me figure out what was going on with him. We all were making money some way somehow and he shouldn't have had any cares in the world. I tried talking to him to figure out what was wrong with him, but I would always get yelled out and told that the only thing that I should be worried about is making money and to mind my business. Me and Fire had been dying to ask him what was going on, but I had learned over time that once he starts snapping and flipping to leave him alone and I did just that. Once we where all packed and caught up on our sleep we were ready to go.

Cash had drove the whole way down and left the car that I was using in Brooklyn. He said that we would only be there for about a month and it was no need for us to have two cars. We checked into an extended stay room in Greenville SC and waisted no time getting to work. "Yo there is a strip club open during the day for yall to work in. I need yall to get dress and get to it."

We had gotten sleep on the way down but that still didn't mean that we were ready to work. Me and Fire looked at Cash and I was tired and had no choice but to ask, "Why are you so pressed for money lately? What's going on? Can we at least eat and relax?' Of course, Cash flipped. Literally. Before I knew it the table and chairs where flipped over and Fire and I had had a few things thrown at us out of anger. "Bitch why the fuck is you asking so many questions. Didn't I tell you to mind your fucking business. But since yall want to know we lost the apartment in Brooklyn so if yall don't make no money we are homeless."

Fire and I just sat on the corner of the bed in fear, disappointment and confusion until Cash stormed out of the room. Little did I know, that would be my last time seeing him for a long long time. She looked at me with her mouth wide open and asked what we were both thinking. "Did he just say we lost the apartment in Brooklyn? Yo Joy I don't know what's going on but every since yall came back he hasn't been acting right. We been making mad bread Joy and he told me that he had been paying the rent. Something Is not right, and I got a bad feeling about all of this."

Fire was just as pissed off as I was. "Joy I left mad shit in that apartment. He could have told us before we left that we weren't coming back." We sat there and talked about the situation for what seemed like hours. We both were trying to figure out what was happening. Had Cash started doing drugs? Was he tired of us? We both had so many questions. But being that we both were in love and blindsided by this man we were willing to do anything to make sure he was happy again. Even if that included losing sleep and not eating until he was satisfied. "Look, lets just post on Back Page and catch some dates off there and from now on lets just get money and let him figure this shit out with our living situation. The apartments and shit are cheap down here and it shouldn't take us long to get out of this hotel." "You right Yo let's just get some money. That way he won't be so uptight when he gets back."

Even though Fire and I had a good idea, we were both wrong. After we both showered, I posted a quick back page add for two girl specials. It was only the afternoon and we both could make a quick $300 if we hurried up and caught the lunch rush. I had never worked in Greenville but knew that it couldn't be any different than any where else. At least that's what I thought so anyway.

The phones started jumping and before you knew it our first date was on his way. "Joy for some reason I'm nervous. I don't know if it's because I haven't smoked but I don't feel right." I was feeling the same nervous feeling as she was but brushed it off. I just want to make some money to make this man happy. I was tired of the way he had been acting and treating us lately and I just wanted it to change.

A few moments later there was a knock on the door. Fire opened the door as I stood behind her and we were met with a tall handsome white man dressed in black slacks and a white polo shirt and dress shoes. He stepped inside the room as me and fire got to work. "Hey baby what's up, how are you? You got the money? You ready to have some fun with us?" For some reason he looked disappointed. "Um, I think I'm going to pass ladies. I gotta get back to work." I had another date set up and didn't care that he changed his mind. I figured that he was nervous, and this was his first time. Fire and I were both dressed in head to toe red thong sets and looked good, so I know he didn't turn us down for the way that we looked. "You want to leave baby you sure?" He shook his head yes and I got up to open the door for him.

He ran out of the room and before I could close the door all the way I turned around my heart fell to my feet as the door was pushed back open and I heard, "Freeze! Both of you don't fucking move." Fuck! That's the only thing that had been going through my head as me and Fire stayed quiet and got hand cuffed and looked at each other. There were about four detectives in our hotel room. "You ladies came all the way from NY to get locked up for prostitution isn't that a shame. Hey light skin where is you all's clothes at, so we can go ahead and get you both downtown and booked. Hopefully yall learn your lesson and go home once the judge lets you out."

I had a feeling that I wasn't going to be let out. I was way to close to NC for them not to extradite me back for my warrants and I was right. After the detectives threw whatever clothes that the could find on me and Fire, they tossed our room looking for drugs and guns and took us both downtown where we were booked, and I learned that my unlucky running streak had ended.

Fire and I had seen a judge within a matter of hours. She was released and had to come back to court about a week later. She came out of the video court room smiling, "Joy I'm out of here you if they keep you you already know we coming to get you. You should be straight thought right?" I just looked at here with tears in my eyes. I had known different. While I was getting booked and after my finger prints came back my arresting officer kept it real and told me that I would be sent to NC. I didn't want Fire to panic so I kept my mouth closed hoping that the judge would see that these warrants were over four years old and by gods grace would let me go home.

On another note I was tired. Tired of running. Tired of having to put up with all that I had been through just to have somewhere to lay my head. Tired of being raped and robbed and taken advantage of. Tired of the game and having someone that I had fell in love with pimp me for their benefit and not caring about me. Tired of not having anyone to talk to and understand me. Tired of late nights and risking my life for money. Tired of having sex with random men every night. God must have known that I was ready to give this game up and was tired of it all and used this to wake me up and get me away from it all.

I walked back out of the video court feeling both relieved and scared. As expected, I was being released from SC, but I wasn't free. Within a few hours I was in the back of a Guilford County sheriff's office van. I was being extradited back to where it all started for me.

CONFESSION AND TIP NUMBER NINETEEN:

WHEN GIVEN A SECOND CHANCE TO START OVER, DON'T GIVE INTO THE LIES AND DEMONS OF YOUR PAST LIFE AND NEVER EVER GO BACK!

I found myself facing everything that I had been running from. I had been locked up for three months waiting for a court date and had not heard a word from Cash. I had been through so many emotions from everything that I had been through up until this time and was ready to accept whatever fate that I had to face.

I was sentenced to 1 ½ years for malicious conduct by a prisoner and embezzlement. The judge did not add any extra charges for me running while on probation, so I ended up getting kind of lucky. On top of that I didn't have to be on post release after my sentence was complete.

I was sent to North Carolina Correctional Institution for Women in Raleigh where I served my time alone. I struggled my whole bid. I ended up having to once again do whatever I had to do to survive. I had been locked up plenty of times before and had to use what I learned in the streets to survive in prison. Like the rest of my bids I stayed to myself but this time that didn't work. I found myself in fights and being sent back and forth to seg. I was still kind of miserable and mad that I had gotten caught not to mention the fact that I hadn't heard from Cash in over a year.

I had only one friend that looked out for me when she could. I was miserable but this time around I wasn't lost. I eventually accepted the fact that I had a second chance and probably would have ended up dead had I not gotten locked up. Only god knows the relief I felt.

I got myself together the best way that I could and stopped getting in trouble and picked up reading and working out. I put together a small plan in my head that I would stick to reading and working out until my release. I also got my GED while I was there and had gotten closer to god through prayer.

A few months before my release I had gotten a long letter from my mom that included two obituaries. Both of my grandmothers had passed away. Her mom and my dad's mom. My brother had twin babies and my sister was doing well. The rest of my family was ok and had been happy that I was ok even though I was in prison. My mom eventually came to see me, and we talked and cried my whole visit. I was happy to see her despite all the bad things that has happened the last time that we seen each other and the fact that I had missed out on so much with our family. My mom didn't even want to know anything that I have been through in the streets but welcomed me back with open arms and was allowing me to come and stay with her once I was released from prison.

This was amazing news to me. Now I didn't have to worry about where I would be going. I was able to have a fresh start at life. This would allow me to get close with my family and use their help and support to stay focused get a job and go to college. Hopefully I would be able to come home to the family and love that I had always wanted and needed.

My family and I were in somewhat contact the rest of my prison bid and I had even started getting letters from my dad. I had stayed focused and had read 100's of books and even lost 60 pounds from working out everyday and Yoga. I was in shape and I was focused on a better life and couldn't wait until I was out of prison and with my family.

I knew that I was suffering mentally from all the things that I had been through and promised myself that I would go to a psychiatrist and a therapist to help me heal and forgive. I was released three weeks after my 22nd birthday in October of 2012. It had been a long 18 months but much needed.

"Welcome home sis !!" My mom had came and gotten me from prison on the day that I was released, and we pulled up to her new three-bedroom two-bathroom house in Charlotte NC.

I had heard good things about Charlotte while I was locked up and couldn't wait to see what the city had to offer.

My sister was standing on the porch jumping up and down waving balloons around being the silly, goofy funny girl that I had remembered. "Oh, my god look at you! You look good! Look at all this hair you lost so much weight.!" "No look at you girl you haven't aged a bit since the last time that I had seen you." It was so nice to finally be back with my family. We sat and talked and had even cried for hours. I had promised them that I would get a job and stay out of trouble no matter what. My sister gave me some money to go and get some clothes with and eventually had to leave and go back home to go to work.

After she left, my mom and I sat in the living room and talked, and she helped me put together a plan. The next day, I would be going to the DMV to get a ID, and she would be taking me to at least ten places to fill out job applications. She had caught me up on what's been going on with our family and I was shocked to hear nothing but bad things. My mom was still moving around from place to place and other than my brother having twins my family was still separated and struggling.

The conversation ended up reminding me that I still had resentment towards my family for them leaving me all alone and in the streets for years, but I dismissed it and promised myself that I would save it for therapy and stay focused on my new plan.

A month had passed by and I still had not found a job and the strip clubs and sugar daddies were calling my name. My mom and I started arguing again and I begun to get stressed out and lost hope. They say the devil comes at you harder when you are at your lowest point and they wasn't lying. I logged into my Facebook account and low and behold, I had a message waiting for me from Cash. He had given me his phone number to call him and I waisted no time grabbing the house phone and walking as far away form the house as possible without losing service to call him.

I had so many questions and wanted to know why he left me stranded the way that he did. What happened to him? Where was he now?

Turns out that Cash had gotten locked up a few weeks after I did for a parole violation and had only been home for about four months. He told me that Fire had left him, and he's been selling drugs for a while and wasn't a pimp anymore. He told me that he couldn't write me or get in contact with me until he seen me on Facebook. We ended up talking and catching up for hours and just like that I was back in love and was yearning to be back by his side.

This time Cash was begging me to come back to him. He promised that it would just be me and him and I didn't have a thing to worry about. Cash promised that once I moved back, I would get a job and only must dance if I wanted to and could go to school as well. He told me that he would support me no matter what and only wanted to be with me and only me.

Things weren't working out for me in NC and I still had a void when it came down to my family.

Cash made the idea of me coming back sound so sweet and by the end of the conversation, he had talked me back into coming back to NYC.

CONFESSION AND TIP NUMBER TWENTY:

IF IT LOOK LIKE A PIMP, WALK LIKE A PIMP AND TALK LIKE A PIMP THEN IT'S A PIMP

Two days later I was saying my goodbyes to my family and once again on a one-way bus to NYC. This time I would make it count for everything that I had hoped for last time around not to mention the fact that I was going to be back with the only man I had ever loved outside of my father.

I was so full of excitement on the bus that I couldn't even sleep. I couldn't wait for Cash to see me and my new look with all the weight that I had lost. We pulled up to the 42nd street terminal and I was one of the first people to get off the bus. I walked to the intersection where Cash told me to meet him at and as promised he was sitting right there in a gold Acura waiting for me.

"OMG look at you cash. I fucking missed you." He had gained weight in the right places and was looking even better than before wearing his usual Jeans and button-down shirt. "Look at you looking like a starving Ethiopian can I get a hug? Are you hungry?" I could tell that he was impressed with the weight that I had lost, and I made sure that I had worn my best fitting jeans and a nice bright pink tight shirt to show off my new figure and decided to wear my natural hair out.

We hugged each other for so long we started holding up traffic. We realized the traffic and rushed to get in the car. "Where you want to eat at? Applebee's?" "Applebee's is cool. I'm tired though. I was so excited to see you I didn't even sleep on the bus." "No problem after we eat we can head to the house and get some rest. I don't have anything planned until tomorrow anyway." It felt good to hear him say that and not say we must go to work right after.

We parked and headed in to Applebee's. Once we were seated we just looked at each other and smiled. I still had so many questions to ask him but decided to enjoy the moment instead. "So where are you staying now?" "I mean you know me Joy I make a way out of no way. I ended up getting a foreclosed house and cleaning it up and turning on the power. It's a three-bedroom house so there is plenty of room."

He sat beside me and put his arm around me, "But what's up though you miss me? Are you ready to be mines again for real this time?" I smiled and shook my head yes. For the remainder of our dinner we just caught up and reminisced on all the crazy things that had happened in our past. It was crazy how we could now laugh at all the drama that went on and I was happy that it was all over and that we were starting a new chapter on another level. This time we were together as one.

Once we finished our meal we jumped back in the car and headed to our new home in Queens. We pulled up to a town house right on the corner of Springfield Blvd in Saint Albans. I could tell that the house was a bando by the way it looked outside. I figured hell, just if it's clean on the outside who cares.

"Welcome back home." I smiled as Cash unlocked the door. The house was decorated with two brown leather sofas and a brown mini bar in the living room. The small kitchen was behind the living room and hadn't been decorated but had all black appliances. To the left of the door was the staircase that led upstairs where there were three evenly sized bedrooms and one full bathroom.

Cash walked in behind me and closed the door. I looked around and noticed that there were females shoes and a jacket thrown over the arm of one of the couches. I scrunched my face up and looked at him waiting for him to explain to me what this was all about. Maybe he had roommates. "Whose stuff is this?" "That's Jessica and Stephanie's stuff. You will meet them later" "Ok but are they your roommates or something?"

Cash looked at me and seemed to be annoyed at the fact that I was asking him questions. While looking at him some more, I noticed that his whole demeanor had changed, and he had almost seemed evil. "Look I told you that I wasn't going to pimp you anymore, but I got these two girls that I came across in the Bronx that have been staying here. they been here for a few months now. I'm not really a pimp anymore but you know they give me money here and there for me letting them stay here and taking them where ever they need to go." "Cash what the fuck Yo! You couldn't have told me this before I got here? How do you just keep this from me? Did you at least tell them that I was coming back up here with you or did you tell them about me at all? Your wrong for this you know, that right?" "Its not that big of a deal and honestly if you don't like it you can go back home. It is what it is."

I sat there with my mouth open and tears forming in my eyes. I had put my trust back into this man all for him to lie to me. And here I was back into a sticky situation with no money. This time thankfully I had family to call. If needed I would borrow some money and take my ass right back to where I came from. I didn't come back up here for this and I damn sure was smart enough to believe Cash was telling the truth about his 'roommates'.

I looked back up at Cash and shock m head in disbelief. I couldn't believe that he had lied to me. "I want to go back home. Can you please pay for my ticket if not let me use your phone, so I can call my mom and ask her to send for me?" "So, you just gone leave me already and you just got here. I told you its not what you think. Just wait a couple of days so you can see what I'm talking about."

After all the promises that Cash had made on the phone he ended up being the same flip floppy guy that I had hated before. I honestly fell for his lies and thought he had changed. I felt so stupid once again.

There was a knock at the door and in came two girls. Jessica, 19, my height and light skin wearing a brownish red wig with a toned body. Then there was Stephanie, 21, dark skin tall and slim wearing a long black wig. They seemed to be just as confused as I was. "Ladies introduce yourselves." "Hi, I'm Stephanie and this is Jessica." Something did not seem right with these girls. They seemed scared or maybe it was just that they were tired. I don't know what it was, but I just knew that something wasn't right, and I had to get away from here. "Hi guys my name is Dee."

After we said hello we all sat there quiet until cash spoke. "Whenever you ready you can go upstairs and shower. There is a blow-up mattress in the room next to the bathroom where you can lay at." I took this opportunity to be alone and try to figure out a way to get some money and take my ass back home. There was no way I was putting up with this all over again. After my shower I decided to lay down and get some rest. I would work on getting away from Cash tomorrow. If no one would be able to send for me than I would just have to catch some dates to pay for my ticket to get back to NC. I was willing to do whatever it took.

I was so tired that I ended up sleeping all the way until the next morning and was awaken by Jessica knocking on the door. "Hey D do you want breakfast? We are about to order some food." "No, I'm good but thanks for asking. Is Cash downstairs?" She answered yes, and I looked at her and could tell that she had just came from working either the blade or back page. I had known that look all to well. I just shook my head and stayed focused on leaving.

Once I had brushed my teeth I made my way downstairs to and saw Stephanie sitting on Cash's lap laughing and smoking with him. I automatically got pissed off and was mad at the fact that this man had really lied to me all over again. This time I wasn't holding my tongue. "Yo Cash can you please come drop me off somewhere." He swiftly moved Stephanie off his lap and walked up the stairs signaling for me to follow him.

Once we were upstairs, I noticed that he had that evil look inside of his eyes all over again and before you knew it my head was banged up against the door while his hand was wrapped around my throat. "Yo what the fuck is your problem. Don't you see me in the middle of doing something?" I felt hot tears instantly drop from my eyes. "I just want to go home please. You lied to me Cash why did you lie to me?" I stared at him waiting for an answer as snot ran out my nose and tears ran down my eyes. I couldn't believe that this was happening all over again.

"You know what, I see your not the same rider that you were before. Prison done softened you up? Ill make a deal with you. Work for me for two weeks and then you can go home. I'll even let you keep half of what ever you make so you don't go home empty handed." At this point I was so afraid that if I said no it would cause more pain to me physically than if I obliged and said yes. I shook my head "Whatever Yo two weeks and then I'm leaving." I had hoped that I would make enough money within the next few days to just up and leave. If it's one thing that I remembered how to do it was how to run and get away.

CONFESSION AND TIP NUMBER TWENTY-ONE:
IF YOU MAKE YOUR BED REMEMBR YOU MUST EVENTUALLY LAY IN IT. AT LEAST MAKE IT COMFORTABLE ENOUGH FOR YOU TO STAND IT.

A whole week had passed, and I was miserable. Cash reneged on his word and I had never feared anyone as much as I had feared him. He had taken things to a whole new level and I had to put together another plan to get away from him. I felt bad for Stephanie and Jessica because it seemed that they got it just a tad bit worse than I did. We barely spoke to each other and it seemed we all had one thing on our minds and that was how to get away.

He told me that I could keep half of my money to save up to leave and he lied once again. Every day that I had made money he searched me from head to toe to make sure I had given everything to him. He also had been making me work on back page instead of in the clubs as promised.

I found myself crying myself to sleep every night trying to figure out how I was going to get away from this mess I had come back to. I had told myself that I would just leave. I would just walk out while he was asleep and find someone's phone to use and call my mom. At least that's what I had hoped to do. It was an early morning and we all had just gotten done with a long night. I decided that today would be the day I leave. Cash had a parole appointment later and I would do what I had to do to get the fuck away from this madness. I went upstairs and got into the shower and laid down after and patiently waited for cash to leave. I was thinking and rethinking my way out to the point where I had a headache and listening to the conversation that Jessica and Stephanie were having about a stinky trick the night before. Eventually I drifted off to sleep.

"Wake the fuck up and put your hands on your head now!" I jumped out of my sleep hoping that I was having a nightmare. I was surrounded by four police officers all with their guns drawn in my face. "What's going on I didn't do anyt…" "Shut the fuck up and put your hands on your head." I couldn't believe I was being arrested for something that I clearly did not do. I didn't even know why or how the police where in the house.

I had fell asleep with only a bra and panties on and once the officers seen that I was harmless, they allowed me to put on a pair of blue jeans and a t-shirt. Afterwards, the officer instructed me to put my hands behind my back and walk downstairs and sit on the couch.

After I got downstairs I noticed that Jessica and Stephanie had been sitting there as well. After I had sat down I looked at Jessica's face and noticed that she had a swollen lip and eye. After putting two and two together, I figured that Cash had done this to her and she had called the police on him. The crazy thing is none of us were in hand cuffs and I hadn't seen Cash. "Ok ladies I'm going to give each of you a chance to explain to me what's going on here." "Officer I don't know. I was sleeping in my bed and yall came and woke me up. I have no idea." "Ok how about you two ladies which one called the police and who is this guy in the back of the squad car?"

We all looked at each other with the answers in the back of our throat but knew better than to let it slip past our lips. "Ok everybody up your all getting booked." "For what! I didn't do anything! I don't even know what's going on!"

We all were cuffed and individually put into the back of three different squad cars and of course were taken to the prescient that knew me the best. 113th. As soon as I walked inside I almost vomited at the familiar smell of dirt and must. We were all placed in a holding cell and were pulled out for more questioning one by one.

I wasn't worried about going to Rikers Island or even getting booked. I hadn't done anything, and I was almost certain that if I explained thaw I had just gotten back to NY that I would be released.

A detective came and pulled me out of the holding cell and into a small room. He sat me down inside of a chair and asked if I wanted a cigarette or something to drink. I declined and began explaining before he could get his first question out. "Detective I don't know what's going on. I woke up and got arrested." "Is that your story and your sticking to it?" "Yes, sir because I didn't do anything." "I don't even know why I'm being arrested." "Well right now we are trying to figure out who this weed, and gun belong to that we found inside of the house that you were sleeping in." "Its not mine sir." "It seems like that's what everyone of yall are saying. So right now, you are getting booked for possession of a firearm and possession of a narcotic."

I immediately started crying. I had been out of prison for a little bit over a month and was already going back to jail for shit that didn't even belong to me. I couldn't help but to cry as I heard all the mental I told you so's play back in my head. I got angry with myself for listening to Cash and believing that he cared for me and believing all the lies that he had told me to lure me back into his arms.

The whole time I was getting finger printed and even on the way to central bookings I cried. I eventually got a head ache and started throwing up from the pain. The whole time that we were in central bookings I noticed that Jessica and Stephanie hadn't said not one word to me or each other. I was curious as to what happened to Jessica's face but had been in so much pain and heartache that I left it alone. I had never cried so much in my life.

I cried all the way up until we finally reached that third cell and my lawyer called me into that small room to speak to me. "Hello Ms. Marshall, you and our co-defendants are being charged with possession of a narcotic and fire arm. Is there anything that I need to know? I see you have a lengthy record of prostitution and you have never had any other charges. Hopefully the judge will look at this and see that these things didn't belong to you or your codefendants and let you all go. But they may decide to remand you and set a small bail for abut $500 only because you have a lengthy record. Is there anyone that you want me to call to come and get you incase they set a bail?" "No" I had no one to call. I knew that my mom didn't even want to hear it and cash was locked up right along with me.

I took my chances and prayed that I would walk out of this courtroom and take my ass back home and never even think about NYC again. But, I had another fate, "Set bail for Marshall for $10000. The other two are ROR." I couldn't do anything but cry as I was escorted back to the holding cell to wait for transportation to go to Rikers Island.

I sat there for about an hour before two detectives came and told me to stand. This was new to me. I had never been transferred to Rikers by a detective before. "Ms Marshall we are detectives from the prescient and we are here to rebook you. You are now being charged along with your boyfriend and co defendant with Sex trafficking as well as a possession of a fire arm and possession of a narcotic. You have the right to remain silent…." The detective read me my rights as I almost passed out and zoned out. I was praying that this was a dream but it wasn't. This was my reality.

Somewhere somehow, I was being blamed for sex trafficking not only myself but two other women on top of possession of a gun and drugs that weren't even mind. Never mind the fact that I had just came home from prison. I stared at the detective as he continued to read me my rights. It felt as if though I was paralyzed and deaf. I couldn't hear a word or even move my legs as they dragged me back to the front to get rebooked for serious shit that I didn't even do.

CONFESSION AND TIP NUMBER TWNETY-TWO:
WHILE LOCKED UP, BELIEVE HALF OF WHAT YOU HEAR AS WELL AS HALF OF WHAT YOU SEE

It was the beginning of January and I had been on Rikers Island for a whole month and had been to court twice. Both times that I have been I didn't even get to see a judge and my bail had went from $10000 to $150000. I hadn't heard from my family but had seen Cash at court. I was so distraught and couldn't believe what was happening to me. I cried every day. I had never felt so lonely and so lost in my life.

As usual I kept to myself and the only thing I did was read and mind my business. I couldn't even get a job while I was in jail because of my level of offense. I had no one to be there for me and no support what so ever. I was still confused as to why I was even locked up in the first place. I had seen the craziest things while locked up and heard the wildest stories. I had heard everything from the facts of other people's cases to horror stories that involved CO's and inmates that were happening right in front of my face and I had no clue.

As the days went by, I had gotten more and more depressed. I woke up every day starring at the old grey brick walls of the small and the grey metal doors of the building that I was in and eating the stale food from the mess hall and dealing with the attitudes of both CO's and other inmates.

I eventually gained some type of sanity and just let go and started socializing. I met a girl named Sparkles that had befriended me. Me and sparkles had become close over the past month that I was on Rikers. She was locked up for the same thing that I was locked up for and we related to on another level. She was a breath of fresh air for me. She was someone that I could talk to about anything and she checked me every time I found myself crying or getting depressed about being locked up. She had been there for over a year fighting her case and I prayed to god that that wasn't my fate. I had never been on Rikers that long and didn't think I could handle it.

I haven't seen or heard from my lawyer since the day that I was arrested and had no idea that my case had gone public until a Spanish lady in my building told me she had heard about me on 1010 wins. I already knew that whatever it was, they were lying.

After all I had been arrested for a bunch of stuff that I did not do so they more than likely were going off what someone else had lied about.

"Yo why this lady just told me that she heard about my case on 1010 wins." "They did the same thing to me when I got locked up. They be lying like fuck. Don't even worry about that. You ready for this spades game later? I need to win me some food." "I looked at sparkles and laughed. If it was one thing that she always had and didn't mind sharing it was food. "Yes, girl I'm ready. Lol" That's all I did every day that I woke up. Eat, showered, played cards, read and worried.

My next court date wasn't until another month, so I did whatever I could to make myself comfortable while I was in Jail. Cash had written me and had given me his friends phone number to call and relay messages through him if needed. His friend was also a listening ear for me. I would call him on the days when I didn't think that I would make it and between him and Sparkles, they would always know the right things to say and gave me hope that everything would be ok.

I had gotten use to being around Sparkles every day and was depending on her to help keep me sane. But of course, with the luck that I had been having lately............ "Marshall pack your shit your being moved" "O shit bitch I think they are about to put you in building 11. You gone be good there! They got cigarettes and everything there." "What

Sparkles what the fuck I don't care about that I don't want to be moved! I want to go home." "Yo I'm telling you your going to like it over there."

I shook my head and grabbed the large garbage bag that had been given to me to put my little bit of belongings in. I hadn't had any packages, but Sparkles had given me some clothes to wear of hers that she had outgrown during her bid.

After I was packed up, I stood in line to be escorted to my new building. I walked in the hallway with the escorting officer until we reached building 11. The metal gate opened and as soon as I walked inside to walk to my cell I felt nervous. It seemed like everyone was staring at me as I walked with my head down to my cell upstairs on the second tier. I finally reached the inside of the small cell and was surprised to see that it was already clean but that didn't stop me from using the Sani wipes that Sparkles had given me to re wipe. Afterwards I unfolded the thin green mat and made my bed and decided to stay in my cell and read for the rest of the night.

For the next few mornings I woke up, ate breakfast and went back inside of my cell. I didn't even bother socializing with anyone. From what I had seen so far while in line for meals is that you could pretty much do whatever the fuck you want in this building. It was if there wasn't an officer there and the inmates did as they pleased. Whatever system they had was working because there was no arguing, and everyone seemed to get along and was calm. But then I remembered sparkles telling me that they had cigarettes so that explained the calmness. Hell, I didn't give a damn. My court date was coning up in the middle of February, so I was just going to continue to mind my business and I did just that.

One morning I woke up and did my usual routine and came out for breakfast. They were serving cold cereal and fruit, so I knew that the line would be short, and I would be able to take my food back to my cell if things had changed. I stood in the breakfast line and noticed that there were about five or six inmates crowded around the officer's desk. I looked and noticed that the officer, a short middle aged stocky man had his cell phone out and was letting the inmates watch you tube on his phone. With everything that I had seen so far while on Rikers, I wasn't surprised. If anything, I was curious and wanted to watch some videos.

I grabbed my breakfast and made my way to the back of the crowd to see what the hype was all about. I bobbed my head to the music as I watched the video with everyone else. Once the video was over, the officer glanced over at me and it seemed as if though he was starring. The way that he was looking at me made everyone turned around to see what he was looking at and they were met with my blushing face.

A few of the inmates had left and went back into their cell once the music was turned off. I turned to walk away but was stopped. "Hello. How are you? You're the new girl in 32, right? What's your name?" I smiled. "Yes I am. My name is

Darcell." "My name is Sam. I work overnights. What is a pretty girl like you doing locked up?" Did he just call me pretty out loud? "It's a long story and I'm sure that you don't have time to hear another story." "I have about an hour left. Pull up a seat and come and talk to me." I stood there wondering if this was some sort of trap or if he was being nosey. He had to had been won of those correctional officers who were cool with all the inmates and gossiped about everybody.

I was trying to stay as low key as possible. I didn't need all my business out there. But of course, my curious ass took a seat anyway. "So, what are you locked up for?" "I got arrested for sex trafficking." "O you're the girl that I had been hearing about. I heard that they are trying to give you like 10 years. I was reading an article about you earlier today look." He pulled out his phone and showed me an article that was posted online about my case. I grabbed his phone and felt so disgusted about all the lies and allegations that was written about me. "Wow this is so fucking crazy. They don't even know what happen this is some fucking bullshit!" I went into further explanation to him about the case and my situation. "Yea I know. That's how it usually goes. But hey it's about to be count time. Ill be here tomorrow if you want to talk." "Ok. It was nice meeting you and thanks for showing me the article."

I smiled at Sam and watched him stare at me as I walked away from him and went and locked in my cell. I couldn't believe that I was being hit on by a correction officer. I guess all the stories that I have heard were true.

The next morning, I woke up and hit my usual routine. Brush my teeth, wash my face and get myself ready to grab breakfast. As soon as I hit the metal staircase to walk off the tier, I glanced to my left and saw Sam starring at me once again. This time he was sitting all alone. I got in line and grabbed the beige plastic tray that held my sorry excuse for a breakfast and was waived over to by him to come and sit with him. I took the fruit and milk off the tray and discarded the rest and sat next to him as requested.

"Good morning Darcell. I think you are so pretty. I can't stop starring at you." Ok self. You were not tripping yesterday. I smiled before replying, "Really? You think I'm pretty?" "Yes, I do. I love your eyes and your lips." (Wait a minute...) "I would love to see those beautiful lips wrapped around my dick" I sat there across from this man with my mouth literally wide open. Did he just tell me that he wanted me to suck his dick? Is this some type of set up? Who sent him? I wasn't sure and all I could think about was surviving.

I finally closed my mouth and smiled with my infamous blush, "And what are you willing to give me to make that happen?" He got a little closer but just enough to not seem obvious to those that were only about twenty feet away from us. "Ill give you whatever you want name your price." Bitch hurry up and think fast. Fuck if it's a set up we are both in the wrong. "How's $100?" "That's not a problem. I'm sure it will be worth it." "Ok so whenever your ready just let me know." "Ill be ready for you tomorrow. But you must promise me that you will not tell anyone. I don't do this, but you are irresistible." "Why would I tell anyone. I need this money more than you know."

"Look, be up for third shift tomorrow. When the captain makes her rounds I'm going to pop your cell. Just meet me over here but make sure you are quiet." My hands started sweating and I started to tremble from being nervous. "Ok. I can do that. That's if you are serious." "O I'm serious. I know you said that you were going to court soon. Don't forget to remind me to give you my number and address. If you get out don't hesitate to call me. I'll be in the Dominican Republic for vacation, but I'll have my phone with me and my daughter will be home if you don't have anywhere to go." I blushed. But it was a real blush this time.

I really felt the sincerity that he had for me and my situation and couldn't believe that he was opening his door for me. We said our temporary goodbyes and made more promises to keep things quiet. I shook my head at my luck all the way to cell 32.

It was 10:30pm. The shifts were about to change, and Sam would be at work in any minute. I had slept all day to rush the time and now I was wide awake, standing at my cell door waiting for him to past by and do his count and give me some type of signal to let me know that we were still on. I heard his keys and shoes jingle and stomp as he walked up the stairs and watched him make his rounds.

Once he was at my door, he stopped and smiled and gave me a small wave and give me the wait signal and I knew that he was serious. I had about two more hours to wait until the captain made her rounds so I decided to jump into a new book that I had borrowed from the dayroom to keep me busy.

As time flew past, I couldn't help but to think that I was being set up. All the what ifs and what nots quickly flew out of my mind as I heard the pop and buzz of my cell door being opened. I took some deep breaths, wiped my sweaty hands on my jeans and slowly opened my door. I looked inside of the bubble and seen Sam signaling me to be quiet as I tip toed down the cement stairs on the side of the building. I walked over to the officers table and stood there with my hands nervously in my pockets waiting for him to come.

Finally, I saw Sam walking around the corner with a huge smile on his face. He got closer and reached for a hug and I obliged. I couldn't help but to smile to hide my nervousness. "Hey sexy, we are going to go in here." he pointed to an empty cell that was used for storage. I followed him inside the stale cell. With every step that I took, I felt my knees and legs get weaker and weaker and my stomach flip harder and harder from being nervous. Was I really about to trick off with a correctional officer?

Once we were inside the cell we stood face to face in an embrace. "Did you bring the money." He smiled and held his finger up to his lips with one hand and pulled five twenty dollar bills out of his pocket with the other. He put the money in my hand and I immediately dropped to my knees, unzipped his pants and did what I was paid to do. Three minutes passed by and he finally pulled his uncircumcised dick out of my mouth and ejaculated all over the floor while I sat back and wiped my mouth with a smile. He looked at me after wiping up his mess with nearby tissue whispering in ecstasy, "That felt so fucking good. Here put this paper up once you go back inside your cell. We got to move fast. Ill see you in a few. Make sure you come out for breakfast, so we can talk." I got up off my knees and put my money in my bra. And just like that, my life had changed once again for the worst.

CONFESSION AND TIP NUMBER TWENTY-THREE:
NEVER EVER BE SO STUPID IN LOVE THAT YOU FALL IN LOVE WITH THE ENEMY, AND EVEN IF YOU ARE LOCKED UP, ALWAYS STAY IN A HOES PLACE

"Marshall, go to inmate assignment." I looked up at the bubble confused from the disgusting lunch that I was trying to eat. Why was I being called to inmate assignment? To my understanding that I couldn't get a job due to the high classification of my case. I guess GOD had other plans.

It has been two days since I had experienced the unthinkable. I was left wondering if Sam really cared about me or was just offering an extended hand for his own personal purpose of pussy. I cleaned up after myself and ran to my cell and made sure my face and breath was in check before heading down the stale smelling hallways to inmate assignment.

Once I was there, I was met with yet another attitude having officer, "Sign in and have a seat." "I was called down here......." "Are you hard of hearing? I said have a seat." Here we go with this again. These Co's had to have been the nastiest most miserable people that I have ever came across. As soon as I sat down, "Marshall, there is a SPA job available in building now for the afternoon shift do you want it?" I looked at her in shock. SPA was a position that paid $30 a week. One of the highest paying and sought-after jobs on Rikers. Of course, I wanted it. I had no idea how I was able to get it, but I took it anyway. It's not like I couldn't use the money. "Ok, when do I start?" "You'll start tomorrow. All you got to do is walk around every fifteen minutes and make sure nobody trying to kill themselves." I was barely holding on to myself how the hell was I supposed to do that? But, for the money, anything. "Ok I can do that. No problem." "Good, that's all. You can go back to your housing area now."

The next day I woke up and hit my usual routine. Shower, hair and dress. I grabbed some lunch and headed over to building 9 which was conveniently located next door to my housing building. As soon as I stepped inside, I that this would be a challenge. No one had told me that this was the housing unit for the mentally challenged. I mean, it smelled like pure shit! On top of that, there were about four inmates standing on the walls banging their heads, others were sitting in chairs rocking back and fourth and then there were the ones inside of their cells yelling, screaming and crying. I shook my head. "Hello, you must be the new SPA." I looked to my right and seen a Spanish CO sitting at the officers table. I looked upstairs and noticed another one. "Yes I am. So where do I sit?" "Let me see your ID so I can log you in. Your going to sit over there." She nodded her head towards a table that was sitting right underneath the staircase.

I gave her my ID and took in my surroundings in discus and said a small prayer thanking god that I wasn't this crazy. After the officer repeated the rules and instructions that I had heard yesterday, I took my seat at the table and decided to catch up on some reading while I was sitting there doing nothing.

"Hi SPA. Do you have food?" I looked up to find that I had been surrounded by the worst smelling people that I have ever came across. This was sad. "No baby I don't have any food. Did you guys eat lunch?" "O Ok. Bye" Uhhhh did I just get dubbed? It was cool with me.

The rest of the day went by quickly and I thanked god that I got through it. I had heard war stories that these inmates where known for smearing and throwing shit at you when they were upset or having an episode. I hoped that I never had to see or witness that. I wouldn't know what to do. Around * pm, I signed out with the officer that was on duty and went back across the hall straight to my cell to grab my things and wash away the day.

The next few days had gone by slow and it finally came time for me to go back to court. I guess it was because I was anticipating both my court date and Sam's return. I couldn't wait to see if my innocence would be proven and if I would be going home. But just in case I wasn't, I had already prepared myself for the worst.

I woke up and got myself dressed and went through the entire tiring process to board the bus to be taken to the Queens county court house only to be told that my case wouldn't be heard today. I didn't even get a chance to see or speak to my lawyer. This was complete bull shit. I was so fed up with this crocket justice system. I had been locked up for almost three months now and I have only seen my lawyer twice and had gone to court four times for no reason.

Once I was back on Rikers Island, I went straight to my cell and cried. I couldn't believe that this was my fate. I was tired, and I was pissed at my self and Cash for putting me in this predicament knowing I had just came home from prison doing time in NC. All I could do at this point was cry and pray and that wasn't enough. I felt myself starring at the grey cell walls wondering if I should just kill myself. There was no way that I would be able to spend fifteen years in prison for something that I did not do. All the thoughts started spinning in my head. Loneliness, heartbreak, confusion, all had taken its toll on me as I sat there crying and thinking of ways to end this all and eventually fell asleep.

"Pssst. You awake?" I looked up to find that Sam had popped my cell open and was standing right over me. "Get yourself together and come downstairs. I'm going to leave your door open." I smiled, "Ok. Give me a few." I don't know why I was so happy to have seen him.

I quickly got myself washed up and headed downstairs. As soon as I hit the corner to sit at the table where he was at, I was met with a long hug accompanied by I miss you and sorry that you didn't go homes. "Yea I didn't even get a chance to see the judge. But it is what It is. I don't even want to talk about it. I have a headache from crying so damn hard." "I swear your to pretty to be in here. But look I brought you some gifts. I have more but I wasn't sure if you would still be here." he reached in numerous pockets and pulled out candy, chips, soda, perfume, gum, lip balm and lip gloss and a pair of bright pink Panasonic headphones.

I looked at him wondering where the hell was I keeping this damn contraband at. "Don't worry about the headphones. Just stay lo key and no one will bother you about it. Don't be afraid to talk to ne about anything that you are going through. I am here for you." "Yo look at these dope ass headphones! Thank you so much for all of this. Lol. You must have known that I was hungry. What's up with the chap stick though? Are you trying to say that I have chapped lips?" "No. I just want you to keep them ready for me when so when I kiss you they will be nice and soft." "Is that right!? What else are you expecting me to do for you for these gifts and how was your vacation.?" "You don't have to do anything for me but keep smiling. Ill bring you the rest of your stuff in a few days. I got you a journal and a note book, so you can write me. I want to know and make sure your days here are ok and I want you to write me when I'm not here, so I can stay informed."

As black as I am, I'm sure you could see me turn red by how hard I was blushing. I looked at him cheesing for the next hour or so as we talked about his vacation and Ex-wife. Is this what it was like to have unconditional love and to have someone care for you and about your wellbeing even though you were locked up and had fucked up most of your life? I wasn't sure but, I was loving this feeling and joy that I was experiencing for the first time in a long time. It felt good to finally have that from someone. Especially in the circumstances that I had been in.

For the next few weeks Sam and I had gotten close. So close that we had became noticed and people started to talk about us and ask questions, but we were both so caught up neither of us cared. I couldn't help the glow that I had from him. I had received so many gifts and attention from him it made me almost forget about the drama that I was dealing with about my court case. I no longer felt lonely. I had him and he had me. I had been back to court with the same results but didn't care and I had even switched my shift to work overnight so that I could be with him while he worked.

On his days off, I would do as he asked and write him long letters and kept myself busy reading the books and magazines that he had given me. Everyone starred and whispered about me when I walked through the halls, but I didn't care. I knew that there was a code of silence and even the Co's who were speculating wasn't bold enough to break it. On occasion I would get a few haters who looked at me and rolled their eyes. Sam had me spoiled with both attention and care. Even though he was a correctional officer, I still felt as if there was hope for a relationship for us outside of this jail shit. They couldn't keep me locked up forever. There were days were I just could not believe that I had him in my life and found myself getting jealous, wondering if there were others. But he didn't even care when I started tripping. He always reassured me that I was the only one he had ever been with as far as inmates and my dumb gellable ass believed him. Until I got a rude awakening.

CONFESSION AND TIP NUMBER TWENTY-FOUR:
ALWAYS REMEMBER, EVERYBODY HAS A MOTIVE. INCLUDING YOU.

"What the fuck do you mean I better suck your dick? Or what? Exactly what are you going to do to me Sam? I already told you I don't feel like it. Plus, you've been acting real strange and distant lately. What happened? You can't wait for me or something? Your tired of me already and moved on?"

"See there you go with your mouth. You like to argue I see. After all the shit that I've been doing for me you can't give me no head? That's what I get for being nice."

I couldn't believe that Sam and I had been arguing back and forth for a week straight. The past few weeks had been rocky with us. I had been to court to find out that they were wanting prison time from me, and my Co defendant had placed a lot of the blame on me with our charges to save his ass.

My world had been crashing once again and the small hope and happiness that I had with Sam was beginning to faint away. We had been arguing almost every day because of the lack of communication. Suddenly, he had stopped bringing me gifts and speaking to me.

There were even a few nights that he didn't even want to talk to me. He would tell me that he was tired and wanted to sleep his shift away. But here he was asking me to suck his dick after he had distanced himself from me. "So now you're going to throw what you have done for me up in my face? That means that you didn't do it from the heart. Is that what this was about the whole time? Sex? Really?" "Whatever Darcell. I don't need any more stress right now and your stressing me out." "Why don't you just talk to me? Tell me what's going on? Why have you been so distant? What's stressing you out?"

I stood there in front of a man that I had fell in love with, with tears in my eyes realizing that it wasn't stress that was causing him to act the way that he had been acting not ready to except the fact that he had been using me this whole time and he was now tired of me. I wasn't ready to give him up just yet. He had been to good to me and I was willing to do whatever it took to keep him and get him back to the way things were before. Even if that included sucking his dick when I didn't want to.

With tears in my eyes, I took the initiative to walk to the slop sink and open the door. "You know what, Your right. I shouldn't be adding stress to your life. Let me make it up to you. Come here. I'm about to give you the best head that you have ever gotten in your life."

"Marshall, pack up your being moved!" I stepped outside of my cell once the door had been buzzed open. I was being moved? My first thought was someone had told someone somewhere about me and Sam. My second thought was that he had gotten me moved. How was I going to see him now other than work? I was still bothered by what had happened the night before. I couldn't believe that our relationship was standing on its last legs and the fact that I didn't know why was killing me.

I had done everything I could to keep us a secret and not betray his trust in anyway and had done everything he asked me to do. I shook my head and thought about anything that I had possibly done or missed to try to figure out why this was happening as I packed my stuff. I had been moved to the 500-bed dorm area and I couldn't have been more pissed. Not only was I losing Sam I had lost the little bit of freedom and personal space that I had with an individual cell.

I looked around the huge room that was filled with 50 beds and 49 other lost women of all different nationalities. I unpacked my stuff as I was approached by a thick Spanish girl, "Sparkles said meet her in at rec today she needs to talk to you." I looked at her, "Ok. What time is reck in this building?" "Its about to be in like a half hour and they will leave you if you're not at the door. I'm not going, don't worry ill look out for your stuff."

I smiled thinking to myself yea right. I got myself together and stashed my stuff the best way that I could and waited by the front door to go outside once rec was called.

As soon as I stepped outside the door, I saw my friend sitting on a concrete stoop. "Yoooooo what the fuck is going on Darcell? I've been hearing so much shit about you and Sam. My nigga you're not low you need to be careful. People know what's going on and he will try you." I gave my friend a hug and began to let everything out. I told her about everything from Sam suddenly flipping, me being moved to my court case. I took full advantage of the short time we had together to talk to her and use her for an open ear. I had been keeping all this stuff inside and needed to let it out.

Once I had spilled my guts out, she looked me I my eyes, "Darcell listen to me. I was in this same predicament and you need to know that you are not the only girl that Sam has and is sleeping with. He is known for this. Did he give you any cigarettes to sell?" "No but he's giving me other stuff and my dumb ass had the nerve to suck his dick after he flipped on me." "OMG darcell no! He is using you mama. That man doesn't love you baby girl. This same thing happened to me but because I didn't have any evidence when I told on him no one did anything about it. Don't let him make you have sex with him."

Sparkles went on to open my eyes. Unfortunately, I had begun to realize that she was right. I was being used once again a now being played with. "Look, the next time he makes you have sex with him or tries to make you feel guilty enough to have sex with him this is what you do, when he cums, make sure you take his cum and put it on you somewhere. Try to put it inside of your pants or your bra. That way you can have some proof of what's going on. You need to be brave and tell on his ass so this stop. Hes going to keep trying you Darcell. Its going to get worse from here. I know your sad and depressed with all of this but you gotta be brave and stand up for yourself. You don't want to be found hanging in a cell dead and they are claiming its suicide when he really did it to you." Our conversation was cut short once rec had ended. I had left my friend feeling scared that what she said was true and was hoping that Sam wasn't that type and didn't take things that far. After all I still loved him, and I would try and talk to him at work that night to see if we could work things out.

"You told me that I was the only one that you have ever done this with. Why did you lie? You really used me for sex?" He looked at me with blood shot eyes and I could tell that he had been drinking. He stood up and before I could react his hands was wrapped around my neck and I couldn't breathe. "What the fuck are you doing talking about me to other people. Who told you to come back over here anyway. Didn't they move you? Since you want to bother me get in there and bend over."

Sam took his hands from around my neck and I felt paralyzed. I couldn't move because I couldn't believe that sparkles were right. This man had been faking this whole time. I busted out in tears, "I'm not getting ready to fuck you. Fuck you. I don't mean shit to you. This whole time you fucking played me. I'm not fucking you no more and you don't have to worry about me bothering you know more." "You're not fucking me no more? Don't play with me. I will get you fucked up. You don't want to fuck with me like that Darcell I promise you that you will regret it."

The fucked-up part about all of this was that he was right. I knew that he had the influence to make every threat that he had just said to me happen with a snap of his finger. I was alone. No one to call. No one to care. Realizing that, I turned around once again with tears that I was tired of crying in my eyes and bent over.

Two days had passed by and I hadn't slept or eaten anything. I was sick. I was depressed. I was once again alone and lost with no one to turn to. Not even a clue about what to do. Being that I was in a dorm I couldn't even cry. I was numb. Holding this all inside. I had even stopped going to work. I couldn't stand to be anywhere near him. I just sat on my thin green mattress and stared at the ceiling. "Hey your name is Darcell right? The officer in building 11 told me to tell you that you need to come back to work." I looked at this girl to numb to even reply. I just shook my head and wondered why in the hell was Sam sending messages through inmates? Didn't he know that he had caused me to be depressed and once again confused? "Thanks, you mami." But maybe he finally wanted to talk and work things out. Maybe just maybe he had loved me after all and was just going thorough a tough time at home. I decided to get up and get ready to see what it is that he had wanted.

"Welcome back to work. Where you been?" I smiled at the Co who worked overnight. "I had needed a few days off." "O Ok just know I can't allow you to go back next door anymore. Its nothing over there that's going to benefit you anyway." O shit. Its true. People did know. "What's going on with you case?" "Same old shit. They are going down on the time though. They offered me 5 years at my last court date. Of course, I didn't take it. I didn't even do anything but that's another story that I don't even feel like talking about." "Ok if you need to talk I'm here."

I went and sat down at my table after making my rounds. I looked to my right and saw that Sam was standing in the pantry that connected the two buildings. I walked over there disregarding the looks that I was getting from the officer and walked inside of the pantry with Sam.

"Here. Take this. I am so sorry for everything. I didn't mean to out my hands on you. I've been so stressed out lately and I've been taking it out on you." Sam placed a bag of tops tobacco in my hand along with some candy and some more lip gloss. "I didn't have any money to give to you, so you can sell this for whatever it is that you need. When the captain makes her rounds make sure you come back so we can talk." I gave him a long hug and let out a sigh of relief. He finally was coming back around.

After the captain made her first rounds I walked back through the unlocked pantry door and met Sam at the officer's desk in building 11. I reached to give him a hug and he pushed me away from him. "What happened that fast we were just good a few hours ago. You got an attitude already?" He didn't even say a word. He just got up, unlocked the slop sink and looked at me as if I was supposed to just walk inside and let him fuck me again. "Stop standing over there looking dumb. You think I gave you those cigarettes for no reason or are you going to come in here and pay me back." "I'm not fucking you for no fucking cigarettes your bugging." "Darcell don't fucking play with me get the fuck in here. I'm not going through this with you again." "Yo Sam what the fuck is wrong with you. You lost your fucking mind. I'm not fucking you anymore!" "Darcell I can get you fucked up and you know it. Do you really want that? After everything that I've done for you……" "Here you go trying to make me feel guilty again. Yo fuck you Sam."

All the emotions that I had been having had came back and tears had once again flooded my eyes. I couldn't believe that this shit was happening once again. I stepped into the slop sink promising myself that this would be the last time. Sam stood in front of me, unzipped his pants, pushed me to my knees and stuck his dick in my mouth. I cried as I was on my knees. "Stop all that crying and open your mouth."

The conversation that me and sparkles had popped into my head. I had to do this. I had to be brave. I had to end this. As soon as he ejaculated, I spit his semen out and did as I was told. I reached inside of the gap jeans that I was wearing, the same pair of jeans that I had on when I got arrested and rubbed all his semen on the inside of my jeans. As soon as I did that. I stood up. Looked him in the eyes, told him fuck you and walked away for good this time.

Once I went back next door, I asked the Co to allow me to go back to my housing unit. I noticed that he could tell that I had been crying but I didn't care to explain. He gave me a hall pass and as soon as I reached my dorm I grabbed my things and headed for the shower. I sat under the shower for a while crying in once again disbelief. Is this what life was about? Heartache after heartache? Was I really that dumb to where people knew that I would be easily taken advantage of? Why did these things keep happening to me? What did I do? What was I going to do with those jeans? Could I really tell on a man that I still loved despite what was going on? Could I see myself possibly putting him behind bars? After my shower I wiped my face, got dressed, picked up the jeans and carefully wrapped them up with the cigarettes that Sam had given me and put them in the bottom of my bucket. I had needed to talk to sparkles immediately.

The next few days were a blur for me. I couldn't sleep, and I didn't know what to do. I couldn't eat. I couldn't even talk hell I couldn't even feel. I decided to go back to work but this time during the day just to get out of the dorm. Plus, I was supposed to meet up with sparkles and for us to have the same rec time I had needed to go with building 9.

I still had the cigarettes that Sam had given me and had planned on giving them to someone to sell for me for commissary. I knew that our relationship was over but I my case wasn't, and I still needed to survive while I was locked up. I decided not to chance going outside with them on me, so I put them in an empty cell that was used for me to go to the bathroom while I was at work. I used the few minutes to call Cash friend to speak to him for a few and turned around and saw that one of the inmates had gone inside the cell and took the cigarettes and given them to one of the Co's and was pointing at me and I knew that she was telling on me. "Fuck" is the only thing that was going through my mind. Shit was about to get real and I knew it.

CONFESSION AND TIP NUMBER TWENTY-FIVE:
WHEN SHIT GET REAL, REMEMBER TO KEEP IT REAL WITH YOURSELF AND WHO YOU ARE, OR YOU WILL LOSE YOURSELF. IF YOU DO FIND YOURSELF LOSING YOURSELF, YOUR FUCKED

I was escorted out of building 9 by security and surprisingly it was back to my dorm. Security had taken the contraband from me, wrote me up and the only consequence that I was facing was being moved to another dorm. Word have traveled fast as usual and by the time I reached my new dorm I was bombarded with questions from inmates. I didn't even have time to take all of this in and figure shit out.

"You're the girl that just got caught with the rollies right?" "You got anymore?" "Yo you were fucking that officer from building 9?" "You dint get in trouble for that shit you must have been telling." I just looked and rolled my eyes and was happy to hear my name being yelled from the bubble. "Marshall go inside of the cafeteria." Saved by whoever it was wanting to talk to me.

I walked inside the cafeteria to find three huge men with badges on sitting at a table staring at me. Fuck. I done fucked up. They ended up being from Gang Intelligence. They had asked me a million questions and interrogated me for over three hours. I couldn't get up to use the bathroom or anything. I still felt as if I loved Sam and by the end of the interview I had told them that I got the cigarettes from an officer that I had only met one time. I felt like complete shit but also knew from what sparkles told me that they probably weren't going to do anything to this officer anyway.

"You had us in here for three hours to tell us that. Girl we didn't give a fuck about that. We just wanted to make sure you weren't a gang leader. You could have been said that." OMG. These people aint shit. "But we do need to move you though, so I hope you didn't unpack. We are putting you back in building 11."

Did he just say that he was putting me back in building 11? Yes! At least I can finally be back with my baby. Hopefully all of this was happening for a reason and we could finally talk and work things out. I was smiling on the inside as I grabbed my things and followed the officers down the hallways back to building 11.

They gave the officer in the bubble my card and escorted me to my cell. This time I was on the bottom tier. I noticed that I was getting a lot of negative stares and o shits from the other inmates. I brushed it off. I already knew that they were talking about this whole incident.

The officers left, and I decided to go to use the phone and was approached by the CO that was working the afternoon shift. "No maam. I was told that I could not let you come out of your cell by security. Please don't ask me any questions and please just go back inside of your cell. They will come and get you and explain when they get the chance." I walked back into my cell with my head down in disbelief. Here we go with this shit.

I sat on my bed and tried to figure out what was going on and I heard a knock on my cell door. It was one of the inmates. I walked to the door, "Why the fuck would you tell on that man for? Sam took good care of you and you done told on him. What they must have put you back in here to spy on us or something." I looked at her and rolled my eyes, "I did not tell on him what the fuck are you talking about." The officer called the inmate over to the officers table telling her to leave me alone.

Is this what everyone was thinking? That I had told on Sam? Little did they know it was the complete opposite and I was trying to protect him. I couldn't believe this shit. Hours had gone by as I sat on my bed waiting for security to come and let me out my cell.

Dinner had passed by and I wasn't even allowed to eat nor was I offered any food. Day had passed, and night had come, and I was still sitting in that cell. I had over heard conversations about me and disregarded the misinformation that was being spread around about me. I couldn't wait until Sam came on shift, so I could talk to him and tell him what really happened before someone else told him lies.

I did what I could to keep my mind from running while I was in that cell. 10:30pm rolled around and there he was. The man that was causing all this heartache and pain in my life. I sat at my door listening to people warn him with lies that I was back in the building. "Yo Sam the put that bitch back in this building. They trying to set you up. She told on you Yo don't fuck with that bitch."

I watched from the inside of my cell as his face showed fear and anger. He was believing them. "Sam don't believe them. They are lying. I promise you I didn't tell on you just come and talk to me." I had no choice but to yell through the door to try and get his attention and it didn't work. He was believing the lies.

My eyes filled up with tears as he walked past my cell without even looking at me as if he didn't even know me.

I stayed up the entire night thinking about everything that was going on. Morning had come, and I still wasn't able to come out of my cell. I wasn't even offered breakfast. I had started to feel sick and dizzy from the stress, lack of sleep and not to mention the fact that I haven't eaten anything. What was I going to do? I didn't tell on him but was being treated like I did. I was stuck.

I sat on the thin green mat and metal bed frame with my eyes filled with tears as all the things that I have ever done in my life had flashed before my eyes. From me being a little girl, being in NY, being in prison in NC, this whole case with Cash, Sam, having no friends or family, being stuck in this cell. I started trembling and noticed that I couldn't breathe. I stood up as all my thoughts came crashing down on me at once. I couldn't make them stop.

I felt like my life had been flashing before my eyes and there was a voice yelling at me in my head. "Shut up! Please stop!" the noise wouldn't stop. I felt my knees go weak as I yelled to the top of my lungs and heard the echo bounce off the grey cement walls. Before I knew it, I had dropped to the ground yelling and pulling my hair as everything around me faded to black.

CONFESSIONS

AND TIPS OF A

BLACK

GIRL ONCE LOST

PART TWO:

STILL LOST

It has been days since I had been transferred from Rikers
Island to Orange County Jail and two days from my last court
date. I still couldn't eat, sleep or function without busting into
tears. All I could do was stare and replay what just happened
in my head repeatedly. I was trying to make some sense out of
my life and what I was going to do. I had a court sentencing
coming up that I wasn't ready for.

Although I didn't see a judge, my last court date consisted
of numerous newspaper journalist and lawyers all wishing to
speak to me. Word had gotten out about what had happened
between me and Sam and they were all interested in hearing
about it, promising to help with one way or another. I was so
caught up, numb and distracted with all the stress from Rikers,
I told my lawyer that I would take the time that was offered.
They were offering me a 1-3-year sentence if I pled guilty.
The catch was that I had to register as a sex offender for the
next ten years.

I just wanted to get out and go home and if taking that time
could allow me to do so then so be it. I couldn't stand the fact
that I was so dumb enough to allow someone to use me to the
point where I broke down mentally and couldn't function. I
still had no one to talk to. No one to call. No one to care. I was
alone, and you would think that by now I would be used to it,
but I wasn't. I needed someone. I needed someone to give me
hope and to help erase the thoughts of me wanting to leave

this earth. I needed someone to be there for me and tell me that I was going to be ok and to help me get back to normal.

"Marshall, go to visitation!" I had only been here for a few days. Who was visiting me. I prayed that it wasn't my family. I didn't want them to see me like this. I was still unable process the fact that I had to be transferred from Rikers Island to another jail because shit got so real.

After washing my face and freshening my breath, I walked downstairs to the bottom tier where there was an officer waiting to escort me to my visit. "Marshall, go to room number 2." I found my way to the designated room to find a young petite white woman with brown hair and grey eyes sitting on the other side of the plexiglass smiling. O no. Not another journalist wanting to talk to me.

I sat down and picked up the phone, "I'm sorry but I don't want to talk to anybody about Rikers." "No no no. I'm not a journalist. I'm a lawyer and I want to help you." Not another lawyer. She should have just sent a letter in the mail like the rest of them. For some reason my intuition told me to look up. I looked up and glanced into her eyes and felt a sense of comfort that I hadn't felt in a long time. "My name is Barbara Hamilton. What happened to you was wrong and I want to help. Someone had written me a letter a few weeks ago explaining to me what has happened to you. I know your in a lot of pain mentally and is going through a tough time with your case. It's going to take some time for you to heal through this pain and you may never get over this and I also understand that you are not very trusting at this point. Darcell I am here to help you. I am more than certain that we can get you some type of money if you wish to proceed with suing not only the officer who did this to you but the city as well. Justice needs to be served."

ABOUT THE AUTHOR

Darcell D Marshall wrote this book with the purpose to never see anyone make the same mistakes that she has. She is also the founder of 'Care and Control Inc', which is a nonprofit with a mission to help formerly incarcerated men and women transition back into the community as smooth as possible.

Contact Information:

Email: Marshall.darcell@yahoo.com

Facebook: @Author Darcell D Marshall